AMERICAN ROYALTY

ROYALTY

By Laura McGehee

THE ROYAL BIRTHDAY

EPIC
Press

The Royal Birthday
American Royalty: Book #1

Written by Laura McGehee

Copyright © 2017 by Abdo Consulting Group, Inc.

Published by EPIC Press™
PO Box 398166
Minneapolis, MN 55439

Cover design by Laura Mitchell
Images for cover art obtained from iStockPhoto.com
Edited by Ryan Hume

LIBRARY OF CONGRESS CATALOGING-IN-PUBLICATION DATA

Names: McGehee, Laura, author.
Title: The royal birthday / by Laura McGehee.
Description: Minneapolis, MN : EPIC Press, 2017. | Series: American royalty ; #1
Summary: The day of King Jonathan George Washington's 65th birthday party can only mean
    one thing. It is time for him to name his successor. While each of the three children scheme,
    double-cross, and posture as best they can in order to secure the crown, Queen Donna
    Franklin sets a plan in motion that could topple the world entirely. The King's decision
    sends shockwaves throughout the nation.
Identifiers: LCCN 2016946187 | ISBN 9781680764772 (lib. bdg.) |
    ISBN 9781680765335 (ebook)
Subjects: LCSH: Washington family (Fictitious characters)—Fiction. | Kings, queens, rulers,
    etc.—Fiction. | Inheritance and succession—Fiction. | Interpersonal relationships—Fiction.
    | Young adult fiction.
Classification: DDC [Fic]—dc23
LC record available at http://lccn.loc.gov/2016946187

EPICPRESS.COM

To absurdity, for keeping us young

PROLOGUE

George Washington took a long, deep swig of mead and basked in the reflective glow of intense adoration from his fellow Revolutionists. They each stared at him with wide, hungry eyes that were consumed with *his* thoughts, opinions, and directives. He had never experienced such complete and total ownership of another's self—not even over his own horse Buttercup, who had become prone to demanding oats wherever and whenever she wanted them no matter the circumstances.

George filled his gut with a deep breath and delivered the punch line that his boys needed.

"And so I said to the King's chambermaid, 'There's a reason they call me the *Sword* of the Revolution, if you know what I mean,'" he said, with a wink and a gesture toward his nether regions. The bar erupted into rowdy cheers and raucous laughter; nobody could tell a joke like Washington, not even Franklin when he drank twelve glasses of wine and insisted on acting in character as Williamsburg Williamson, a hapless British solider with a lisp.

"Another shot of Whiskey Rebellion for the boys!" Washington shouted, which elicited even more cheers. The boys were red-faced, disheveled, and far too drunk to hold the course of history in their hands. Washington regarded them all with an intense feeling of camaraderie that only months of sweating profusely together in a tiny hidden chamber, plotting the future of the nation, could inspire. Hamilton and Adams were in the middle of an ill-advised chugging contest that would certainly end in patriotic pain, Jefferson had pulled his top hat over his eyes and seemed to be sleeping while standing up, Franklin mimed Williamsburg Williamson trying to shoot a gun but accidentally holding it backwards, Madison was on the verge of another deadly illness but proudly pounding back scotch in an effort to cleanse his spirit, and Burr sat in the corner with a dark smile. The bartender passed around shots of Whiskey Rebellion, and the men lifted their glasses high. George smiled at the thick mixture in his glass, and decided that this would be his first item to tax when he was in office; he knew his country could never live without their whiskey.

"To the future President of the new country!" Hamilton shouted loudly. Washington shook his head and refused to raise his glass, shooting a wry smile at his treasured Alexander Hamilton while batting his eyes. The boys *loved* this routine, and Washington loved his boys. They laughingly jostled him and urged him to join in their toast. Washington solemnly shook his head.

Everybody laughed even harder and shouted until their faces turned red, demanding that he take the shot. Washington sternly shook his head once more; as his boys knew, he was great at pretending to be noble. When Hamilton leapt onto the bar top and began to sing "We're not throwing away this shot!" with his arms around Burr and Franklin, Washington broke into a beaming grin. Hamilton always knew the way to his heart. He gravely rose to his feet, and the boys immediately quieted down.

"To the best *goddamn* leader you boys will ever have!" he said, with as much force as his gravelly voice could muster. His boys cheered in response. George tipped the abrasive substance down his throat and felt it burn, just as the British had burned in a bright blaze of American glory. He had never experienced pain that felt so savagely empowering, not even when shrapnel had lodged into his right knee during Yorktown.

Washington had discovered somewhere around his twenty-first birthday that the key to success in this world was pretending as if you knew what you were doing. He had been thrust into power as the major of the Virginia militia following his Uncle's untimely demise, and adopted an aloof reserve that stemmed more from his lack of experience than anything else. But as he continued to grow up (quite literally) and silently tower above the rest of his men—occasionally uttering phrases that seemed weighty and wise by their isolation— he realized that being well-liked was simple. To the public, he was reserved, and they assumed he was always deep in thought when he was often just thinking about dinner. He saved his rowdier moments for the privacy of late nights, like tonight's eve of celebration on the cusp of determining the course of history.

They had worked hard for years to get to this point, and had spent the past few months in a caged prison of heat-induced insanity in that godforsaken hidden Pennsylvanian meeting room. After all of the screaming matches, debates, and thinly veiled threats on each other's families, they were poised to sign the Constitution tomorrow and give birth to a new nation. Washington thought it was time for some good, old-fashioned, drunk American unity. Also, he had been restricting his drinking to only eight drinks a day during the Constitutional Convention, and he thoroughly missed the warm buzz of copious amounts of whiskey flowing through his veins at all hours of existence.

At six feet two inches, George stretched over the rest of his peers like the oldest tree in a forest. His distinguished nose and chiseled jaw imbued him with the sort of power that seemed pre-destined, and he had spent his whole life in the endless pursuit of greatness. He looked down into his wine glass and was startled by the soft splash of his wooden teeth. He quickly shoved the set back in his mouth and darted a glance around to make sure nobody had noticed. Luckily, they were busy arguing about Alexander Hamilton's idea to turn the traditional duel into a battle of dance and song.

"I'm telling you guys, it would be an incredible way to prove who is the best through wit, stamina, and the crafting of breakaway hits of self-expression!" he said, his eyes bright.

"I am not dancing," Jefferson said staunchly. "No matter what."

"It thurely would be a thupid, thupid uthe of time," Franklin lisped in that silly presentation of Williamsburg. "Which meanthe that I, a thupid Brit, fully thupport it!"

"Oh, hush," Hamilton said with an eye roll. "It's the future, I promise. They'll all be talking about our musical duels for centuries."

"What's wrong with the normal way of dueling?" Burr asked from the corner, swirling his whiskey.

Washington chuckled and shook his head. This

sort of debate would only end in drunken wrestling, which he simply couldn't stomach with all the Whiskey Rebellion sloshing around his gut.

"Well, I best be going home," Washington said gravely to the room at large, working hard to move his thick tongue in accurate articulation. As he lurched to his feet, the entire bar groaned and shouted protests.

"Just eight more thots, that's all I athk!" shouted Franklin, who was now inexplicably shirtless and dancing with a coatrack.

"Your last night as a free man! The party is just starting!" Adams said from his apparent slumber in the corner. The men rallied around George, and the bartender handed him another shot of Whiskey Rebellion. George smiled at the flushed faces surrounding him, and used the excuse he knew would work.

"Sorry, fellas. I have to go . . . show my lady the Sword of the Revolution," he said with a wink. One by one, the boys broke into beaming smiles.

"You dog!" Hamilton screeched, thumping Washington on the back.

"This man just cannot, and will not, be stopped," said Madison. The men would not let him leave until he gave them all the very top-secret Freemason handshake, which had the distinct possibility of becoming less and less top-secret the more they shouted about it in the tavern late at night. But Washington performed it expertly, finishing with a flourishing tap of his Square and Compass engraved ring against his fellow Freemasons' hands. He stumbled out of the bar into the night and the crisp September air.

He walked over to his trusty steed, Buttercup. She had been with him for years, and he trusted her as much as he trusted his boys. Come to think of it, he probably trusted her more, because she had never even once tried to dip his fingers in warm water while he was sleeping to make him pee his pants.

"How you doing, honey?" George asked. Buttercup sniffed his mouth and then blew air out angrily. She pawed the ground with her hoof and shook her mane in frustration.

"I'm sorry, really, they wouldn't let me stop," George said. "But let's just go on home."

He clambered up the side of Buttercup and struggled to swing his leg over the saddle. As he teetered on the edge of the horse, gravity bested him and he toppled back down to the ground with a sickening thud. Buttercup neighed and reared her head, shaking her head definitively. George lay on his back on the ground and stared up at the clear night sky for a few moments before reluctantly rising to his feet. He eyed Buttercup once more and could not exactly bring her blurry figure into focus, no matter how much he tried to squint.

"Alright, alright," George finally muttered under his breath. "Maybe we best walk." He grabbed Buttercup by the reins and began the three-mile trek back to his home. He knew he couldn't afford to get another drunk-riding charge, not when he had a country to lead. He walked through the shadowy streets, savoring the crisp air that could only mean fall was around the bend.

By the time he arrived home, he had walked a good amount of the whiskey out of his system, and it felt a lot less like he was going to lose the contents of his stomach at any moment. He brought Buttercup into the stall, remembering at the last minute to tie her up correctly. Martha would have his head if she woke up to find the horse in the kitchen again, calmly munching through their stock of fresh oats. He tiptoed in through the back entrance, hoping that Martha would be fast asleep and he could slide in next to her without waking her. But he tentatively opened the door to find Martha calmly sitting at their kitchen table with a glass of wine, a constantly flickering candle, and a hell of a lot of legal scrolls.

"Hello," Martha said.

"Hi," he said, and then began to giggle. He couldn't help it; the Whiskey Rebellions had certainly taken their toll. Martha's dark eyes softened and she emitted a few giggles of companionship.

"What's so funny?" she asked.

"I'm going to be President tomorrow," George said. "I'm going to be the most important man in the entire world." Martha responded with an even louder laugh, and before long, the two were clutching their stomachs and crying tears of laughter. George felt his head swim with elation, and he thought that this was quite possibly the happiest he had ever been. After a few moments, their full-bellied laughs subsided and George sat down with Martha. He poured himself a glass of wine, which made Martha raise her eyes.

"I didn't drink *that* much," George protested.

"I could smell the whiskey from a mile away," Martha said.

"Well, I didn't drink that much wine," George

clarified, taking a sip and smiling. "I think this is a time for celebration, don't you?"

Martha nodded and raised her glass to meet George's.

"We did it. All those years and all those . . . sacrifices," she said.

"If that housemaid wanted to keep her ears, she shouldn't have used them to overhear our conversations," George said.

"My thoughts exactly," Martha responded.

"To us," George said.

"To us," Martha agreed. They clinked their glasses together and drank the sweet red wine.

"And the paperwork is all . . . taken care of?" George asked, his eyes darting to the family trees and adoption papers scattered on the table in front of them.

"They'll be filed tomorrow. Nobody will ever know," Martha said with a smile. George felt the rush of cool relief flood through his veins; he could always count on his wife. After a few moments of luxurious contemplation on both their parts, George asked another very important question that had been on his mind for quite some time.

"Do you think my face would look good on a mountain?"

After a few more glasses of wine and long discussions about the correct scale with which one should be carved into a mountain side, George and Martha retired to their bedroom. Within a few moments he was deeply and truly asleep, his dreams taking him to a world that even he couldn't imagine.

He slept fitfully during the night, living a fugue state that shattered his reality in ways that not even the Freemasonic spiritual retreat, induced by healthy portions of mushroom pie, had managed. His dreams were chaotic, vivid, and governed by a meandering narrative that did its best to communicate a sense of youthful recklessness and search for identity, despite its occasional lapses in structure and clarity. He awoke in a cold sweat, even before Farmer John's rooster sounded the morning alarm, unsure what had been real and what had been a dream. He shook Martha awake.

"What? What is it?" she asked groggily.

"Are you real? Is this real?"

"It's too early for existential crises," she mumbled into her pillow. George propped himself up and rubbed his pockmarked face to make sure it still felt the same.

"What if we could have more?" he asked.

"For the last time, we already have three horses, George, we don't need any more."

"No, that's not what I mean, Martha! What if we could have more of *everything*, and there could be one supreme organizing force that would let us retain control over everyone under our domain. What would you say?"

"I don't know what you mean," Martha said, rolling over on her side. "You're still drunk."

"Well, of course I am, but that's beside the point!" he said. He jumped out of bed and ran to his closet to throw on his nicest trousers and shiniest vest. He knew what he had to do. He kissed Martha a quick goodbye and ran past his manservant Bishop, who thrust a warm sweet bun into his grasp for good measure. He saddled Buttercup and settled his stomach with the sweet bread, steeling himself for the riot he was about to induce.

Washington stalked silently into the back of the nondescript assembly hall that he now knew better than his own reflection. He had spent hours pacing up and down these creaky floors while listening to his colleagues yell, argue, and insult. Now the very document they had risked their lives for was resting on the front table, shining in the morning light. The rest of the Convention members nervously chattered throughout the room; the air was charged with the electricity of change.

William Jackson shuffled papers around on his secretarial table, and then banged his gavel with a resounding clang. Unlike the rowdier days of full-fledged debate, the crowd immediately silenced. Every delegate stared expectantly at Jackson, waiting for the beginning of the end of the beginning. Jackson tentatively cleared his throat.

"Today we will be finalizing our draft of the Constitution of the United States of America," he said with emphasis, as if expecting a gasp or two from the audience. Unfortunately, most of the men seemed as if their heads and livers had taken quite a beating the night before. When his declaration only found measured silence and a few groans of pain, he cleared his throat and continued, "Mr. George Washington, your opening remarks?"

George nodded, rose to his feet, and felt the eyes of forty-four delegates from across the country intently trained on him. He slowly walked toward the front table, and swiveled to face the sea of expectant faces before him. He looked down at the document on the table, a truly beautiful piece of legislature. He looked back at the men eagerly awaiting his signing. He cleared his throat.

"My brothers. I think we have made a grave mistake."

A chuckle or two rang out in the back, but George did not smile. The room fell into dead, terse silence. George took a deep breath.

"Our country must be led by a king. And that king will be me."

His voice reverberated around the room, and for a few seconds, everyone stared silently back at him. Then, James Madison rose to his feet.

"Get him out of here! He's still drunk!"

He didn't know why people kept stating a simple truth as if it carried the weight of an accusation. But with that, the room erupted into chaos.

Delegates screamed across the room at each other, and George watched silently from the front of the room. In spite of the deafening madness, a small smile spread across his lips. This was the way it was supposed to be.

CHAPTER ONE

King Jonathan George Washington tore into his fifth cinnamon bun of the morning with anxious gusto. Today was supposed to be a monumental day, and yet here he was, eating more cinnamon buns than Doctor McGilson "recommended" and struggling to remember his Royal GlassPhone™ password. He typed every password he could fathom, from "RoyalfamilyisNumberOne!" to "GeorgeWashingtonForever" to "Worldsbestking69" and none of it worked. With a yell of frustration, he threw his phone against the wall, momentarily satisfied by the resulting shatter. Within a few moments

Bishop steadily marched in to dutifully retrieve the phone fragments with a dustpan.

"I need a new phone, Bishop," the King mumbled.

"I figured, sir," Bishop answered, pulling out a shiny new GlassPhone™ from his pocket. "There was a new model released just a few hours ago, your Highness, straight from Dawn®Glass™ herself."

King Jonathan picked up the phone and lifted it toward his face, but before he could figure out what was happening, the phone flew out of his hand and smashed against the ceiling.

"The phone is weightless, sir," Bishop said. He dug into his pocket and produced another one. King Jonathan shrugged, and opened his phone frantically to the RoyalChatterStream. He scrolled. And scrolled. And then scrolled some more. His anxiety of being disconnected slowly quelled, replaced by the anxiety of reading all of the many thoughts and opinions the American populace had on the Royal rule. But he needed the GlassNet™ to survive—how else was he supposed to know that his vastly pro-truding belly was widely agreed upon by political pundits and peasants alike to have crossed the line from "jolly" into "slightly repulsive"?

After a few moments of intense scrolling, he found what he was looking for, what he always sought when connected to the Stream.

@JonathanLuvr452: Is any1 else sad that the sexiest king EVER is retiring today?

His heart fluttered and he scratched his expanded belly absentmindedly. King Jonathan George Washington was a portly, gray old man who looked more like Santa Claus than the average mall Santa, and hated children even more than the average mall Santa. He had been the dashing young heartthrob type of King back in his day, and he still desperately longed to be that same desirable man. But truth be told, he knew every time he read a disparaging Chatter that his looks had left him right around the time his sons started trending at the top of the

RoyalChatterStream with their own dashing smiles and slicked hair. Now, he was left alone with only cinnamon buns and @JonathanLuvr452 for company. His belly grew with every passing day, almost as quickly as his misshapen beard. There was only one person in the country who still made him feel like he *was* the sexiest King ever, and he had come to need @JonathanLuvr452's validation almost as much as he needed cinnamon buns. He dreamed one day of Direct Chattering back. He scrolled down to see the replies, of which there were hundreds.

@Royalicious222: HELL NO.

@scubaDIVINGsalmon: U r jokin, right?

@TrevorIsMine0003: LOL. Funny.

@GoodbyeMoonPie: So glad we will be gettin a young and h0t king 2nite

King Jonathan felt the strange impulse to throw his phone at the wall once more, but when he looked up he realized that Bishop was still in the room. Although Bishop had bright auburn hair and stood taller than six feet, he conveniently blended into the background of each and every room in the Royal Castle, making him the perfect Royal Butler. His family's service stretched all the way back to George Washington himself, and every single Bishop had looked nearly identical, which led many to wonder if Bishop was actually just a ghost.

"You can go now, Bishop," King Jonathan said, but not before tossing him a cinnamon bun.

"Thank you, sir," Bishop responded. "And happy birthday."

There it was. His birthday. No, not just any birthday, his sixty-fifth birthday. For a peasant, maybe that was a reason to celebrate a well-earned retirement. But for King Jonathan George Washington, he would be forced to name his successor this evening at his Royal birthday party, and he found the prospect woefully upsetting. It wasn't that each of his three children were equally deserving of the post—to the contrary, they were all foolish children who were flawed to the utmost degree. He could not imagine any one of them ruling a Royal HorseGolf leisure league, let alone an entire country.

He wondered if @JonathanLuvr452 was thinking about him right at that moment. He wondered if anyone would remember him after he was gone. He wondered if anyone would care if he ate another cinnamon bun. He sighed, decided the answer was a resounding "no" to all of those questions, and dove into another pastry of sweet-breaded delight.

"King Jonathan?" came the high-pitched voice of Lorena, his secretary. She was an endlessly frazzled young professional, freshly graduated from Peasant Harvard Business School and running the most ceremonial office in the country. Like most of her fellow Royal Staffers, Lorena hoped to work high up in the legislature one day, and had chosen royal grunt work as her path to success.

King Jonathan sighed and swallowed the lump of cinnamon and sugar that had congealed in his throat.

"Yes?" he asked.

"President Wszolek is here."

"Who?" King Jonathan asked.

"The President of the United States of America," Loretta responded in a wearied voice.

"I'm kidding," King Jonathan responded. That was only partially true. He could never really remember how to pronounce her name. W-kolek? W-th-olek? Ws-zolek?

"Send her in."

Jonathan rapidly glanced around his Octagonal Office to assess how presentable it may or may not be. It seemed to be drifting more toward the "may not be" side of things—candy wrappers, comic books, and tissues littered the hallowed halls of his kingly escape. The Octagonal Office had been designed by Dawn®Glass™, Royalty's most cel-ebrated genius tech designer, interior designer, motivational speaker, and elephant activist—responsible for inventing the GlassNet™ and the RoyalChatterStream. The Office stretched high into the sky, located in the center tower of the Royal Castle, and one could view each and every angle of the sprawling Mount Vernonian lawns, and into the Royal Village beyond the Castle walls. But King Jonathan mostly just ate a lot of candy in his underwear and refused to open the blinds.

The ornate wooden door creaked slowly open, and the thin, austere face of President Wszolek looked back at him.

"President," he said curtly, laboriously pulling a robe over his partially unclothed body.

"King," President Wszolek responded. King Jonathan did not understand how a peasant could be so maddeningly casual with a Royal.

"I have three new bills for you to sign off on," Wszolek said. "I assume you don't want to read them." She had short, angular hair, which perfectly matched the severity of her angular jawline. She wore a gray blazer and gray slacks, as she did every day of her life. Her dark eyes shone vividly in contrast to her pale skin, and gave King Jonathan the impression that he was talking to a shark, and in a sense, he was.

King Jonathan merely shrugged in response.

"Great," Wszolek said. "Well if you'll just sign these we can both be on our way." She thrust a collection of papers to the King, and he signed them without so much as a single glance. She grabbed them, turned around, and headed toward the door.

"Oh, Jonathan?" she said as she lingered on the threshold. "Happy birthday." As she left, King Jonathan knew that she actually meant, *I hate you and I am infinitely pleased that you will soon be forced into irrelevancy.* The feeling was mutual, but yet he was still the one who would have to step down. He felt the frustration of a trapped animal and reacted in the way that only a trapped animal could—he stress-ate another cinnamon bun.

"You know the doctor said not to eat *seven* cinnamon buns in one sitting, even on your birthday," came a sharp voice from the conjoining room. Queen Donna Franklin swooped in, rapidly removing her hair rollers and shaking her hair luxuriously.

"Why aren't you getting dressed?" she asked.

"It's eight in the morning," he said gruffly.

"Exactly! We have the next ten hours booked with party preparation!" Queen Donna said. "And you know the George Washington wig takes *forever*." Donna fluttered in and around Jonathan's personal space, smoothing his hair and fussing over the cinnamon glaze on his lips. Donna was characteristically dedicated to preparing Jonathan for the imminent birthday party, despite his best intentions to stay on the ground in his underwear all day. The theme of this birthday party, like all of King Jonathan's birthday parties since age three, was The Boston Tea Party. The Royal invitees could choose from seventeen Royally-produced tea brands, all while floating down the Royal River that surrounded the castle on a fleet of yachts. The entire event culminated in a historical reenactment and the dramatic dumping of crate after crate of tea, which the alligators in the Royal River tended to enjoy.

Parties at the Royal Castle were impossibly grand, once-in-a-lifetime affairs—unless, of course, you were a Duke or Duchess. Anyone who could prove a direct bloodline to one of the Founding Fathers was considered Royal, and those who had been in service to their Court for generations found themselves among the most elite of the elite. A King could only marry a Duchess, which had never proved to be an issue because non-Royals, also known as peasants, had very little to offer. Since the Royalty spent most, if not all, of their time in the Royal Village, there was really no reason to stray into the peasant land of suburban houses and communal schooling that existed just on the other side of the Royal Wall.

"You already missed your false-teeth fitting," she said, with her eyes glued to the schedule on her GlassPhone™. She paused briefly, and Jonathan stared defiantly back at his wife of ten years. He would rather sell the country to Sweden than dive into the party preparation that his wife insisted upon. Although she was gifted with the charming spirit of a bloodthirsty prehistoric creature, the likes of which modern man could only ever hope to respectfully live alongside, she had the looks of a mild-mannered daytime talk show host. She was plump, and often found smiling broadly with kindly sparkling eyes. But her greatest weapon was the fact that looks can be deceiving.

"You haven't picked a successor yet," she accused, as she fixed Jonathan with her powerful gaze, the same one that demanded he get out of his birthday-induced funk and pretend to smile.

"What! No, of course I have . . . " But he trailed off, simply lacking the energy to continue. Queen Donna could see through him like a ghost with an empty stomach.

"They're all idiots, honey," he moaned, dropping his head into his hands. "How can I pick one of them to take care of the country when they can't even take care of themselves? I mean, of course I should pick Trevor. Everybody has always picked the oldest. My father, and my father's father, and my father's father's father, and well, so on. But I'm not sure that Trevor knows how to read."

He looked up at Donna, hoping she would debate that statement, but she just remained decisively silent.

"Plus he's high all the time. *And* I think he probably has a few non-Royal heirs speckled throughout the country. And he's an asshole!" He picked up the pace as Donna merely stared at him without refuting any of his biting statements.

"So then there's Kyle. Sure, a great choice for a volleyball coach or maybe a traffic director, but that boy will change his mind three thousand times in one minute, depending on who is talking the loudest. He's just not King material, and certainly not old enough to rule! He can barely handle puberty, let alone international affairs with foreign dignitaries!"

King Jonathan turned to face the absurdly large

family portrait hanging in the center of the room. It featured the members of the Royal family perching on Royal horses in the fields of Mount Vernon. King Jonathan wore his ceremonial crown and robe and Queen Donna sported an elegant sparkling dress and an equally sparkling smile. In front of them were the two boys—Trevor, equipped with a shaggy beard and a look of painful disinterest, and Kyle, sharply adorable with an alarmingly chiseled baby face, but seemingly in the process of falling off his horse. Standing on the ground with her arms crossed was the middle child, a young woman with dark brown hair tightly pulled back into a bun.

"Emma? Sure, she went to Yale Royal, and yeah, she's been dressing up as King for Halloween since Kindergarten. Yes, she's a smart one all right." He turned abruptly back to face Queen Donna. "But there's no way *she* can lead the country. I mean, what, are we going to call her, King Emma? Would her husband be the Queen? I don't think it's even legal!"

He dropped his head into his hands and sighed heavily. "This party is doomed. This kingdom is doomed."

In one swift motion, Queen Donna crossed the room, lifted King Jonathan's head, and slapped him. The force of the blow brought tears to his eyes, and his mind went instantly blank. He made a half-coughing noise, and she slapped him once more. Then, she stared at him for a few long, powerful moments. He felt her deep brown eyes bore into him, and wondered once again how a Franklin could be so powerful. All of the others he knew were lazy, French-obsessed bums who spent most of their time drunkenly spouting to their friends the importance of electricity or trying to be actors. But no, Donna was different. Donna was special.

It had been forty years since, at his twenty-fifth birthday party, she had approached him in the dark corner of the room when he had been profusely drinking beer and aggressively eying the visiting Princess of Slovakia. Donna simply marched directly up to him and kissed him fiercely with no greeting. She had smiled and said, "I'm going to marry you one day soon."

Then, a few years later, Jonathan married Bernadette Adams and together they had Trevor and then Emma. Twelve years later he got divorced, and a few years after that, he accidentally impregnated Camille Jefferson with Kyle. They married immediately afterwards. Six years later, he and Camille got divorced. Finally, Donna's prophecy could come true and the two were wed later that year. Even though her maniacal power had been the driving force behind most, if not all, of his decisions in the past ten years, he often found himself longing for something softer. Something like @JonathanLuvr452. In fact, he sometimes found himself yearning for a different way of life entirely—what would his existence be like if he wasn't saddled with all this responsibility and rule?

"Don't be stupid," Donna said, the sound of her

slap still reverberating around the room. He rubbed his cheek and looked back at her.

"So you think they will do a good job?" he asked tentatively. She laughed caustically.

"Of course not. They're all idiots." She put her arm around his shoulder, and pulled him up out of his chair. They stood in front of the window, watching as the Royal Party Company started to erect the massive fleet of yachts along the Royal River.

"So what do we do?" King Jonathan asked, his heart heavy.

"What if you didn't have to name a successor?" Queen Donna asked, her voice low and her smile suggesting she knew exactly how the future would unfold. King Jonathan looked into her decisive eyes and was overwhelmed with desire for her incomparable strength. He leaned forward and passionately kissed her, and she responded in kind. As their familiar tongues thrashed around each other's mouths and they mutually grabbed each other's body parts with the frenetic energy of teenagers on a diplomatically arranged date, he felt ever so briefly reconnected to his vitality. But then Donna pulled away and pointed out the window. King Jonathan looked to find Trevor sprinting across the lawn in his underwear with a trash bag over his head, and he sighed heavily.

CHAPTER TWO

Prince Trevor George Washington had always been a great athlete, if not the best in the world. He had succeeded in soccer, baseball, football, ice hockey, air hockey, chess, aggressive baton-twirling, and Bikram yoga, just to name a few. He had won each and every match, even against guys that were three times his size. It was just one of the many pieces of evidence that proved he was the best in everything he tried to do. So when he started huffing and losing his breath halfway through his sprint across the Mount Vernonian Lawn, he was more than a little concerned that his body was failing him.

He had spent thirty-two years taking rightful advantage of Royal living, and apparently, the years had started to take their toll. So when he awoke that morning in Duchess Sardine's bedroom and realized that he was already two hours late for his costume fitting, he had to take drastic measures. Unfortunately, he could only locate his underwear and had no time to fully clothe his pale body. So he had gritted his teeth, emptied the nearest trash bag, and placed it on top of his head to create a superhero mask of the smelliest degree.

Sardine had drowsily opened her eyes and emitted a sharp laugh when she saw the half-naked Trevor standing before her, trash bag and all. He was accustomed to waking up mostly naked in Duchess Sardine's room, but she was perhaps the only Royal woman between the ages of twenty and forty-eight that he had not tried to sleep with. Duchess Sardine was Trevor's best friend, and they were prone to spending late nights at the Green Dragon Tavern, consuming a mind-bending mixture of substances that usually led to some sort of clothing removal and passing out in Duchess Sardine's studio apartment in the Royal Village. Luckily, Duchess Sardine lived close to the Castle, and Prince Trevor never had to sneak very far when he had to return home during all of those morning-afters. But unluckily, she was a Burr, and the Royals hated the Burrs ever since the unfortunate 1804 non-musical duel that had extinguished Alexander Hamilton forever. Whenever a Burr's name was brought up in conversation, Royals were prone to shudder, grimace, and mutter, "Burr," in a hateful tone under their breath. For their part, the Burrs insisted that it had been a fair duel, and Aaron Burr had merely been fighting to save his life. Nobody really knew what happened at that meeting in Weehawken, but the fact remained that Sardine and Trevor's best friendship had been savagely torn apart in the RoyalChatterStream since its very inception.

The years of Royal parties, Royal eating, and

Royal lack of exercise had not been very kind to Trevor's physique. So when his heart felt like it would burst out of his chest and he saw his glorious life of elite conquests and charming smiles delivered to screaming fans flash before his eyes, he knew he had to walk. Even though everybody on the lawn had stopped to watch the half-naked bagged man's morning journey, he slowed down and finished in a huffing stroll. He hadn't stretched that morning, so that was probably why his body was revolting against him. When he reached the gate, Bishop simply nodded with a familiar smile.

"Good morning, Trevor."

"Bishop," Trevor said curtly. "Great day to become King."

"The best, sir."

Once he was safely inside the Royal Castle, Trevor removed the bag from his head and breathed in the stiff Castle air, congratulating himself on another stealthy reentrance into his home. Mount

Vernon had belonged to the Washington Family since the 1600s, but it hadn't truly become a home until George Washington assumed control in 1751. He built an estate that housed his family, his plantations, and all of his Kingly possessions, like his possum farm. He transformed the property over the course of his reign with the help of the secretive league of Freemasons. It is rumored that an average of three children on school tours get lost in the Castle every year.

The Castle boasted one-hundred sixteen separate rooms that were all secretly conjoined, ninety-four sweeping hallways in which one was not allowed to roller skate, sixty-five circular staircases steep enough to cause an accidental death, four kitchens with GlassWare™ installed in all appliances, eighty-six Royal horses who never wore socks, three grand ballrooms in which one was allowed to roller skate, and one possum farm. The entire castle was equipped with GlassTVs™, which connected to every GlassPhone™ so that no one ever had to be without access to the RoyalChatterStream.

Trevor paused in the entryway to stretch his tense legs, just long enough to see the latest Chatter on the GlassTV™ in front of him.

@JanetheReporterOfficial: HALF-NAKED MAN SEEN SPRINTING ACROSS ROYAL LAWN AGAIN.

The news story showed shaky camera phone footage of the portly-bellied Trevor running across the grass, and embarrassingly also included him stopping, panting, and then walking the rest of the way. Trevor's inevitable smile at seeing himself on TV was cut abruptly short when the face of Jane Hammond appeared on screen, microphone in hand and cocky smile poised purposefully.

"Jane Hammond with RoyalChatterStream here, and we have just received reports that this naked bagged man is none other than Prince Trevor." The headline now read: *HALF-NAKED PRINCE*

TREVOR SEEN SPRINTING ACROSS ROYAL LAWN, AGAIN.

"That could be anyone!" protested Trevor.

"This in fact, could not be anyone," Jane said gravely. "Let's zoom in on that." The image of the Naked Bagged Man filled the screen. Jane zoomed in slowly on Trevor's shirtless lower back. "If you look closely, you'll see a distinctive tattoo of the Washington Coat of Arms," Jane said. "Next picture."

Now the screen was filled with a photo of Trevor passed out on his stomach in a bed, his tattoo in full display. Jane declared triumphantly, "You'll see that is indeed the *same* Washington Coat of Arms tramp stamp. This naked display is none other than Royal playboy, Prince Trevor, the rumored successor to the throne."

Maybe getting that tramp stamp had not been the smartest decision Trevor had ever made, but to be honest, he had made worse mistakes. For example, that time he released a drunken press release filmed by Duchess Sardine proclaiming that pants were forever forbidden on Royal grounds. Jane reappeared with a satisfied smile. He couldn't bear to look at that face anymore, and it wasn't even because Jane had mercilessly dumped him thirteen years prior. Trevor clapped his hands angrily and the GlassTV™ shut off.

Trevor briefly wondered if the naked stint would affect his imminent crowning, but then decided that was foolish. Nothing he had done had ever affected his Royal status; that was the incredible beauty of his birthright. He was made for this role, and the people loved him. If anything, this coverage would help people realize that he had a fantastic body and a chill sense of humor.

"Sup, Bishop," Trevor said as he waltzed into his chambers—the Royal Butler was always wherever one needed him, occasionally causing Trevor to wonder if they employed a staff of butlers who all resembled Bishop.

"Good morning, sir," Bishop said politely. He

was standing in the doorway holding a warm face cloth, an energy drink, and pain medication. "The usual?"

Trevor nodded and immediately downed the medication and chugged the energy drink in a way most doctors would not recommend.

"And you have a visitor," Bishop continued. Trevor smiled and walked into the room to find Duchess Sardine sprawled across Trevor's bed, GlassPhone™ in hand and her trademark boredom oozing from her barely opened eyes.

"How the hell did you beat me?" Trevor asked indignantly.

"I literally walked," Duchess Sardine answered. "Like, after eating breakfast, too. You really have to work out more."

"Shut up," Trevor responded.

"You forgot your stupid diet cookies," Sardine said, gesturing to a pile of cookies on his dresser. They were Royal Diet Cookies that were infamous for wracking a person's body with debilitating bowel movements and often leaving them several pounds lighter. Trevor was not ashamed to admit he dabbled in Royal Diets; this kind of perfect body did not just happen overnight.

"Do you have any weed?" Sardine asked; she really got to the important matters very quickly.

"Sock drawer," Trevor responded. Duchess Sardine leapt to her feet and dug through the drawer while Trevor postured in front of the mirror and imagined himself with a crown atop his head. His shapely body glistened with sweat in the fluorescent overhead lighting. Trevor had never looked better.

"Today is the day, Sardine. The first day of the rest of my life," Trevor said. "Thank God the Founding Fathers put an age limit on this thing. Time for a new king. A cool king. A handsome king."

"Where the hell did you put it?" Sardine asked, madly digging through the drawer. Trevor shrugged.

"Look harder," he suggested. Trevor continued to stare at his ice-blue eyes in the mirror and imagined them beneath the crown. "You know, my album is going to be dropping soon," Trevor said. "The first kingly rapper and bongo player. It's going to be incredible."

Sardine did not respond, so Trevor continued to mesmerize himself with his own beauty. He had thick, shaggy hair and an accompanying beard that Donna sometimes made him shave off for special events, but he fought to preserve it because he was an artist through and through. This necessitated spending most of his time and a hell of a lot of money on crafting himself into the image of an artist, because how else was he supposed to feel inspired to think about starting to think about creating a masterpiece?

"What makes you so sure you're going to be King?" Duchess Sardine finally asked, her head deep in the sock drawer as she pawed around blindly for the hidden sock filled with weed. Trevor laughed loudly.

"Sure? I'm not sure. I'm positive," Trevor said.

Duchess Sardine did not respond, and Trevor cleared his throat pointedly. "Every king in the entire history of the universe has been the first-born son. Literally every single one. Do you think my Dad is just going to suddenly decide to change the course of history for no reason whatsoever?" Trevor laughed even louder, and Duchess Sardine still did not respond. "Why would you even suggest that? What, you think he would pick *Emma*? I mean, that doesn't even seem legal. Or Kyle? You really think he would pick Kyle?"

The more Trevor spoke, the more a creeping anxiety began to rise up within him. "Why would you say that?" Trevor asked nervously. "Did you hear something?"

"I didn't say anything, and I don't really care," Duchess Sardine responded. "But you definitely do not have any weed."

"What?" Trevor said. "That's impossible." He crossed his leather-encased room. He had forgone a color scheme in favor of a leather scheme, because that's just how unusually obscure his aesthetic was. He had even grown to tolerate the sticky sensation of raw skin rubbing up against warm leather, a sensation that was unavoidable in this room.

"Did you check the back?" Trevor asked as he dug his hand into the leather-clad drawer.

"No," Duchess Sardine drawled. "I checked everywhere in the sock drawer, *except* the back." Trevor rolled his eyes, and withdrew his hand with a shrug.

"Do you think I need new caps?" Trevor asked absentmindedly as he ran his tongue over his eternally aching teeth.

"Isn't it called a crown?" Duchess Sardine asked.

"No, like on my teeth." Trevor had inherited several lovely traits from the Washington lineage, like a towering frame and a boisterous sense of self-confidence. But he had also been born with teeth so weak they could barely even handle a slightly crisp apple.

"Right," Duchess Sardine said. "Isn't that called a crown?"

"Huh," Trevor mused, locking eyes with himself across the room in one of his many mirrors. "Is that so that peasants can feel like Royals whenever they have bad teeth?"

"No, it's so that you can have a consolation crown when I become King instead of you," came a biting voice from behind, the one that always instilled a deep sense of unease in the pit of his stomach. Trevor turned around with a sneer already plastered on his face to find his sister: Princess Emma George Washington. She stood in the doorway of his bathroom, arms crossed and wearing a dress that looked more like a small house than an article of clothing.

"What were you doing in my bathroom?" Trevor asked. Emma had a habit of showing up whenever he least desired to see her, which happened to be most of the time.

"Using the leather shower," Emma drawled.

"Hey, it is *very* comfortable, and you're far too close-minded to ever realize that!" Trevor shouted back. He was very sensitive about the utility of his leather shower, partially because he spent most of his mental energy trying to convince himself he enjoyed the sickeningly damp cowhide smell from the wet leather.

"A pleasure to see you, Sardine, as always," Emma said. "Kill any innocent American heroes lately?"

"Five, actually," Duchess Sardine responded. The sarcasm oozing from the exchange was enough to drown one or two of the Royal possums. Trevor gestured broadly to the door.

"I invite you to leave as soon as you possibly can," Trevor said, "and you know, you better be nice to me while you still can. Maybe when I'm sitting up on that throne deciding the fate of the world, I'll remember my dear little sister."

"I saw that naked sprint. Are you sure they make thrones big enough for you?" Emma taunted, as she walked toward the door.

"I've got a beautiful figure and I'm proud of it!" Trevor retorted. She found his deepest insecurities as accurately as the targeted advertising on RoyalChatterStream. Emma continued to walk out the door, and Trevor stoically turned his head to the side. He wouldn't dignify her with the complete emotional and spiritual attack he could launch right now; he had more important matters to consider.

"She totally took the weed," Sardine said, her eyes barely moving from her GlassPhone™.

"What weed?" Emma asked innocently in the doorway. Trevor eyed his shifty sister's impassive eyes, and knew that Sardine was right, even though his sister had never even smoked once. That was her way—she liked to cause chaos just because it entertained her.

"Give it back!" Trevor shouted as he catapulted his unwieldy body towards his little sister. But despite his overwhelming size and sheer mass, he found Emma darting out of his grasp, slippery like a snake who had been moisturizing. She scratched, kicked, and clawed her way to eventually pinning him down on the floor and twisting his arms behind his back.

"Sardine! Get her off of me!" Trevor screeched. Sardine merely shrugged.

"Not getting involved in that," she responded. Emma twisted his arm even harder, and Trevor felt the searing pain of failure mixed with a skin burn.

"Alright, alright! I'll stop!" Trevor yelled. Emma continued to twist his arm, no mercy in her eyes.

"Say it."

"I said I give!"

"No, *say it.*"

She twisted even harder. Trevor knew what she wanted him to say, because it was what she forced him to say ever since she had become determinedly aggressive enough to overpower him, back when she was six. He hated saying it, but he didn't have a choice. Trevor finally mumbled something inaudible under his breath.

"I didn't hear that!" Emma said.

"Fine! You can be king!" Trevor responded.

Emma continued to twist Trevor's arm, and

Trevor cried out once more. Emma channeled the sort of Washingtonian rage that had made George Washington feared by his enemies and allies alike, and it made Trevor resent his sister to no end. Finally, Emma let go of Trevor's arm and stood up triumphantly. Trevor took a few moments of quiet recovery on the floor before shakily rising to his feet. Luckily, he knew how to handle these situations.

"I was crossing my fingers behind my back," Trevor said proudly. "So it doesn't count."

"You are such a child."

"*You* are!"

They stood an arm's length away from each other, Trevor massaging his wounded arms and spirit. But no matter how many times Emma beat him up, he still had one ultimate weapon, something that would destroy her if used correctly.

"You know," Trevor said slowly. "You would think that a sister of mine with a little secret like yours would be nicer to me."

She immediately reddened. "I don't have any secrets," she said quickly.

"What about that time at the Superbowl Ball last year when I walked in on—"

"You didn't see anything!" Emma shouted, lurching forward and grabbing the unmarked bag of Royal Diet Cookies off of his leather dresser. "And I'm taking these!" She spun around and stomped out the door, down the hallway. He half-heartedly considered warning Emma against the physical destruction of the bowels that would certainly occur after consuming those cookies, but thought better of it. If she was going to be a lunchtime bully, she would have to deal with the consequences.

"So, like, your Dad told you that you would be King?" Sardine prompted.

"I mean, basically," Trevor responded. "Well, he didn't have to. It was implied. Basically. A lot of looks were exchanged."

Sardine shrugged, and turned her attention back to the RoyalChatterStream.

"All I know is that Emma is going to shit horrifically in like forty minutes," Sardine said with an uncharacteristic giggle. The image made Trevor giggle in return. He was going to be a triumphant king while Emma was a poop-riddled mess—what else could he ask for in this life? Maybe just some weed.

CHAPTER THREE

"**F**aster, you maggots, faster," Coach Nena said pleasantly into her headset as she biked at top speed. "Bike like your goddamn life depends on it, because it does! Hey! You there? Yes, the slob in the back? What the hell do you think that is? Do you think you're going to get away with shit like that on my watch?"

Prince Kyle George Washington, the aforementioned slob in the back, was dripping with enough sweat to fill an ocean, and could no longer feel his legs. He was indeed biking like his life depended on it, but unfortunately, his life couldn't handle this kind of physical and emotional battery. He was a recent devotee to Coach Nena's Royal Fitness Regime, which so far had brought him closer to death than anything else he had decided to do in his entire life, even including that day he went skydiving six times in two hours just to try to get paired with that overwhelmingly beautiful skydiving instructor.

Coach Nena had been the head physical trainer for the Royal family and their Royal subjects for years now, and she had the string of infomercials to prove it. She was responsible for every Royal's impressive physical appearance in the past three decades, from Queen Donna's incredibly toned arms at the 2012 Royal Chess Tournament to Michael Adams' six-plus pack abs on the cover of *Royal Playboy*. Even though Coach Nena's voice was as gentle as a cloud, she spat out the toughest, cruelest, and meanest motivational tactics imaginable. Somehow her bizarre combination of utter disgust at the human condition, paired with her calm and polite demeanor had made her the most successful workout trainer in recent history.

The Royal Gym was a sprawling, six-floored structure equipped with the newest workout technology imaginable, from weights in the shape of GlassPhones™ to trick gym-goers into using them, to treadmills that mimicked the sensation of walking down the aisle to the throne to become the crowned ruler of America. From the outside, it looked like a glass-encased dome that one would find in space, or the ocean, or an ocean in space. The entire enclosure was walled with a Dawn®Glass™ original: an exterior that displayed larger than life smiling imagery of whichever Royals were inside the building. Tourists could crowd around the building in intense anticipation of their favorite Royals appearing on the walls—a particularly popular Royal, like Prince Trevor or Duke Tristan Hamilton, would elicit cheers and swoons. At the other end of the likeability spectrum, a Duchess Sardine Burr would make the crowd boo and spit with disgust. From the inside, the walls were entirely transparent, so that the gym inhabitants could be motivated by all of their adoring fans who cared intimately about how tight their butt was or how many chins they had that day.

On this particular morning, Kyle should not have attended Coach Nena's Butt-Busting Bike Brigade, but he had woken up at four in the morning with only one thing in mind, and one person in his dreams: that tan, weathered woman who was almost certainly abusing steroids. He had sneakily escaped out of the Castle before anyone else had woken up, which unfortunately involved diving through the trash chute and riding out with the morning pick up. But when that truck pulled out of the Royal Gates, Kyle jumped out, sprayed himself with cologne, and headed to the gym for his first of many workout sessions.

Kyle had been working out more than seemed advisable in the past few weeks. In fact, the Royal Doctor McGilson had told Kyle: "Stop working out." The amount of cardio he was doing had been proven deadly in certain clinical settings. Kyle certainly did not need the absurd amount of gym activity; his spry eighteen year-old frame was still blessed with the effortless sort of muscle that only very handsome people were lucky enough to retain after they passed the peak of puberty. He was six-foot-four, dark-haired, and blue-eyed; all in all, he looked like each and every Disney prince that had ever sung his way through a love story. There were even rumors that Kyle had been genetically altered in the womb in order to reach true Royal perfection. But, although Kyle was blessed with the sort of good looks that made people always want to make eye contact with him, he was cursed with an overactive, unconfident mind of the worst kind, and a complete lack of comfort or control with his own body. His room and various corridors had to be bubble wrapped for safety when he was a child. In fact, they still were. He had broken both arms in a tennis accident, his nose when he was laughing so hard he fell down the stairs, his ankle when he was showering, and his glasses each and every time he tried to walk in the dark.

He had always been so good-looking that every teenage female (and a fair amount of males as well) immediately gravitated toward him, but he was always so abruptly awkward that they quickly lost interest. He had spent his youthful eighteen years in love with fourteen different women, actually talked to four of them, and only ever kissed one, and that one had been a cousin. He was perpetually chasing the latest love of his life, which meant that he was following them from afar, stalking them on RoyalChatterStream, and sometimes settling restraining orders quietly out of court with a generous settlement.

"Pick it up, you little pieces of shit. My *dead* mother could bike faster than each and every one of you combined," Coach Nena said calmly into her headset as they prepared to bike up a virtual hill, her taut chin jutting out powerfully.

Kyle did not feel well. He had been so nervous at the prospect of seeing Nena's intensely tanned face that he had not been able to eat breakfast, and now he had been biking for six hours. He had taken one look at Coach Nena's overwhelmingly toned arms, her impassively blank face, and her eternally color-coordinated workout gear, and knew in his heart that she was the one for him. He had heard of her for years, but it was only recently when he was up late mourning the ending of his two-week love affair with Herbatcha the Royal Mail Lady, conducted exclusively through winky faces on RoyalChatterStream, that he saw Coach Nena's infomercial. She had spoken calmly and plainly into the camera about the absurdly disgusting state of your body, yes *you*, and how *you* needed to come into the gym this instant or no human, animal, or inanimate object would ever love you again. Kyle was transfixed. Maybe it was the power of her deeply cutting words, maybe it was his broken heart, or maybe it was true love—but

Kyle had signed up for workout classes at that very instant.

For the past few weeks, he had been lurking in the back of every exercise class, hiding his face and struggling not to make eye contact with anyone. As a Royal youth he was entitled to spending his time generally as he saw fit; save for the minimal amount of Royal tutoring, he mostly just pined after potential lovers from afar. He knew that his older brother Trevor had already thoroughly acquainted himself with a variety of Duchesses by the time he was Kyle's age, but Kyle just could not build up the courage to make any sort of move. He was thrilled to his core whenever Coach Nena called him a maggot or a turd or a piece of shit, and he dreamt about her saying that to him over dinner one night.

He had spent three weeks staring at Coach Nena every day from the back of the class, and every single day telling himself that this was the day he would talk to her. But alas, workouts came and went and he could not work up the courage to say anything.

Here he was, on the day of the coronation—if there was ever any day to say hello, it was today.

"All right, you pieces of human garbage," Nena's sweet voice rang out over the huffing and puffing of sweaty Royal subjects. "We only have six more minutes left, but rest assured, they will be the hardest six minutes of your entire life." Kyle gulped. His bike resistance changed as they began to conquer the virtual hill described by Nena as "way too steep to be physically possible." He pumped his legs as best as he could, and realized his entire body was numb. But once he conquered this virtual hill, he could then conquer the metaphorical hill of talking to her. He would saunter over after his stunning physical success, glistening with sweat and the kind of pheromones that made animals attracted to each other. He would waft some of his smell toward her, and she would perk up and look over at him. Then he would smile and nod. She would smile back, maybe even blush. He would walk over to her, extend a hand, and casually utter, "Hey. Prince Kyle."

And then it would be history. She would love him just like he loved her, and they would have a family and a life together. He would cook her breakfast in the morning, after he learned how to cook. Actually, their Royal Chefs would probably make breakfast for them, but breakfast would definitely be involved. She would move into the Castle with them and it would be utterly glorious. Maybe they would even play the infomercial that had started it all at their Royal wedding.

"Five minutes left, you sick assholes, let's get those legs moving or I will see to it that you never step foot in this gym ever again," Nena half-said, half-sang into her microphone. Kyle had no idea how only one minute could have passed when it seemed as if he had lived an eternity of physical pain. He imagined this was what hell was like. No, he *knew* this was what hell was like.

"Four minutes and thirty seconds left!" Nena's voice rang out, and now Kyle knew that she must be a sorceress able to control time at the slightest whim. He looked frantically around at his fellow Royal elite and found them all equally straining with the impossibility of this hill, save for that glistening douche Tristan Hamilton who cheerily spun his head around like a meerkat. "Think about all those people looking at you, staring at you, *needing* you to be beautiful specimens of human perfection," Coach Nena drawled. "I want to see more hustle in the back, or you're going to disappoint all your family and ancestors and you'll never find happiness."

Kyle put his head down, held his breath, and began to pump his legs as hard as he possibly could. This is how she would notice him; this is how things would change forever. But as he continued to push his legs faster and harder than he ever thought they could go, he felt his vision start to blur. He shook his head, focused his eyes back on the form of Nena in front of the room, and continued biking. He biked for what felt like years but knew to be four minutes, because before long, Nena was counting down from thirty and urging them all to bike as fast as they could. Kyle did.

Suddenly and without warning, he saw the events of his life flash before his eyes. He felt nothing but distant interest as he watched himself, four years old, crying for his mother in daycare and only getting a staff of Royal Babysitters in response. He saw himself cry even more when Donna came to pick him up. He saw himself at eight, still crying, and quietly hiding in the corner of the playground. He saw himself attending fundraisers and dances and parties, still softly crying in the corner. He saw Trevor beating him up in the distant corners of the Royal Fields. He saw Emma beating him up in his room. He saw himself falling in love with Hanna, Bernice, Herbatcha, Joanna, Lillian, Charity, Maria, and a few whose names he didn't remember anymore. Then, he saw himself working out again, tears streaming down his face. Man, a lot of his memories involved crying.

It was almost as if his spirit lifted directly out of his body and began to hover above his flailing limbs. In fact, that's exactly what it was like when he floated up to the top of the room and saw, with distinct apathy, his body fall to the ground. He watched as his fellow exercisers shrieked and noticed that it only took the Royal Service an admirable eight seconds to rush to his side. Then, everything went dark. The last image he saw was a vision of his future: Kyle, crowned as the very first Teenage King, with the rest of his family bowing before him at his feet. For some reason, he was naked, but it didn't seem to matter. He smiled, and looked to his left. Coach Nena sat at his side, displaying those toned arms and a beautiful crown on her head, color-coordinated to match her highlighter yellow sports bra.

The next thing he knew, he opened his eyes and found the piercing gaze of Coach Nena staring back at him. He grinned dreamily at first, because of course, this was how every dream of his started. But then, he felt a damp discomfort spreading between his legs and realized he had fainted and then wet himself in front of the love of his life.

"Prince Kyle. Prince Kyle. Can you hear me?" Coach Nena waved her hand in front of his eyes. All traces of her workout demeanor disappeared behind the fear of a Royal injury. Kyle made eye contact with Coach Nena, and blurted out the only thing he could think to say at a time like this.

"I'm going to be King!"

CHAPTER FOUR

"**G**oddamn bullshit. Bull. Shit. Can you believe it? This is *exactly* what I need right now," Emma yelled at the GlassTV™ on her wall. She was standing in a ruffled, frilly, disgusting dress that was uncomfortably bunched up around her waist, and was entirely captivated by the news report on the screen. Jane the reporter stood outside the Royal Gym, surrounded by masses of screaming fans.

"And yes, we do indeed have several reports that Prince Kyle confirmed he would be named successor this evening at King Jonathan's birthday party," Jane said with that eternal serial killer glint in her eye.

"Here I am standing with Duke Tristan Hamilton, also a member of Coach Nena's Butt-Busting Bike Brigade. Now, sir Duke, can you tell us what you saw?"

Duke Tristan Hamilton smiled easily into the camera, and Emma could nearly hear the women swooning across the country. He had stunning white teeth, an obsession with humming, an annoying tendency to speak in questions, and Emma hated him.

"I was just getting my early morning workout on, you know, gotta keep up that fitness, and then across the room—bam! He's on the ground? A few moments later, he says he'll be King? But I did finish my route in record time, I think?"

"Fascinating," Jane said dryly, while screaming peasants loudly proclaimed their eternal love for Duke Tristan. He smiled and waved while Jane cleared her throat restlessly. Emma considered Jane to be one of the most dangerous people in the Royal Village, but at least she also seemed to share Emma's unpopular dislike for the most handsome Duke in all of the land. Duke Tristan was pulled into a selfie with a throng of passionately yelling young gentlemen, and Jane turned back to the camera with that awful sort of reporter nod that truly meant nothing. "There you have it, folks. Prince Kyle says he will 'be King.' Now, coming up next, we talk to the janitor of the gym—"

Emma turned the GlassTV™ off with a hard clap. "There's no *way* they actually picked Kyle, is there? Is there?!" She turned in a panic to her most trusted Royal cat, Brandy. Brandy swished her gray-striped tail lazily and blinked sleepily at Emma.

"Yes, okay, I know he did all that homelessness advocacy work, but that was just because he wanted to sleep with the director! Charity doesn't count if you're just doing it for sex, with a girl named Charity!"

Brandy did not reply, and Emma huffed and turned back to the problem at hand: how the hell was she going to wear any of these repulsive dresses tonight when she accepted the crown? Emma looked more like a hip librarian than a Princess, and at no point in her life had she ever thought she looked good in a dress. She had shoulder-length hair that was dependably neatly tied back, an intense, powerful gaze, and an athletically built frame. She had always imagined herself in some sort of purple tuxedo or a form-fitting jumpsuit when accepting the crown, not a frilled and disgusting mess of cloth.

The King's birthday party was her least favorite day of the year, because her costuming options were insulting at best. Donna was always "Sexy Martha Washington" to Jonathan's George, and so that left "Sexy Maid," "Sexy Betsy Ross," or "Sexy Slave Girl." Emma had been campaigning for an entire year to ban the "Sexy Slave Girl" costume, on the grounds that it was blatantly racist and an entirely mangled approach to handling the troubled history of slavery interwoven with Royal Rule. But the Royals had greater concerns, like Duke Tristan's arms, or whom Shirley Adams was sleeping with (nobody). Emma had Chattered about the issue to no end, but found that her Chatters rarely, if ever, made it to the top of the Stream.

Emma hated Royal functions; she found them tedious and filled with institutional pressure to perform a nebulous script that everyone seemed to enjoy but her. Each and every party, the elite Royals came together and continued to reinforce their privilege, narrow perspective, and perceived right to rule. These parties always instilled a deep sense of unease in Emma, because she found so much of the Royal's way of life and lack of awareness stifling and idiotic, and yet she knew that she would need to continue to exist within this power structure to ever have a chance at making any sort of change in the world.

So she settled on "Sexy Maid" and looked forward to noting all of the "Sexy Slaves" so that she could excommunicate them once she was King. She half-heartedly tried to pull up the frilly mess, sucking in her stomach and wiggling through the armholes, and then gave up in a mad rush of frustration. She tore off the dress as fast as she could, which was not very fast considering all the buttons and ties. She stood defiantly in her underwear and huffed furiously.

"When I'm King, I will make sure that no Princess ever has to wear this kind of shit ever again," she declared to Brandy. "That's a Royal promise." Once again, Brandy did not care. Emma eyed the stolen cookies on her dresser, and felt the strongest desire to eat the entire bag. She knew better than to truly trust anything taken from Trevor, but she had been forced by her stepmother to refrain from cookies for weeks now and she wanted nothing more than to rebel.

She sighed, and turned her back on the cookies with the sort of self-restraint she never dreamed she would master. She hated *those* Royals, the kind that underwent internal surgeries and genetic modifications to enable a steady diet of white wine, sugar, and rice crackers. She had resisted the surgical enhancements at every turn, but still found herself succumbing to the pressure to alter her natural desire for cookies. Emma wondered what her mother would say if she could see her right now, turning down a delicious treat. Sadly, she could not talk to her mother ever again. Not because she was dead, but because she was in Kentucky, where all Royal divorcées were forced to retire. Well, she probably could go see her—but who wants to go to Kentucky? Maybe she should call her, but wasn't even sure her latest GlassPhone™ was able to make calls.

"And I'll make sure no Princess ever has to use self-restraint ever again, also," she added, grabbing the bag of cookies and eating them in a blind fury. As the crumbling concoction of deep satisfaction tumbled down her throat, Emma turned to the task that had been torturing her for far too long: her acceptance speech. Emma had spent just about every day of her twenty-two years waiting for the moment that she would be King. But when she turned five and started Royal tutoring, she learned just what she was dealing with. As a true-blooded Washington, she had been born into the family that had been ruling the country for over two hundred years. As she grew up, she learned how the Popular Hall of Generally Elected Officials (PHOGEO) was in charge of legislation, which was led by the President.

"But then what does the King do?" she had asked Sheldon, her Royal Tutor. And Sheldon had just laughed. From her observations she learned that her father mostly just sat around in his underwear and ate a lot. She learned that the real, effective power lay with the elected officials, not the born rulers. She wanted to be the King that would change that. The King who would take power. The King who would make a difference.

No King had ever chosen a female heir. Although it was technically possible for a woman to be chosen, the leader of the country would be called King, by Constitutional law. How she longed to be King Emma, just to rub it in her ancestors' faces, which were all conveniently on portrait display in the hallways of the Royal Castle.

Her teenage years had been filled with the angst of being characteristically misunderstood as the only Princess of the Royal family. She was forced to dance with each and every Prince who walked across the alligator-guarded Royal River Bridge and through the doors—even the smelly ones. Yale Royal had promised to be the change she needed, yet Emma had disappointingly found herself in the same social circles as before. Emma deeply hated presenting herself to the public, and as a result, the public grew to hate her in return. The gossip magazines and media became particularly cruel to the reclusive princess, but Emma had decided long ago she didn't care. She was going to be a ruler at all costs, no matter who or what got in her way. She looked up at the portrait of President Wszolek staring down at her from her wall. The very first female President was one of Emma's greatest inspirations, and she yearned to become King while Wszolek was still in office, so the two could change the world together.

A knock at her door jolted Emma out of her thoughts forcefully.

"Come in," Emma said, forgetting that she was only partially clad. Bishop's pale face appeared, and he immediately averted his eyes. A soft blush spread across his cheeks.

"Queen Donna would like to remind you that the hour of the family meeting is fast approaching," he said. "The very important one that all family members must be present for." Emma sighed heavily.

"I know, Bishop."

"And she would also like to remind you that you need to be in one of the four gowns she has selected for this occasion."

"I know, Bishop."

He nodded, and left with his head bowed. Emma rolled her eyes, and returned to face herself in the mirror. She finally succeeded in wrestling on the final dress, an elegantly silver number that trailed on the floor behind her. This costume was simply termed "Sexy Socialite." It was certainly the least hideous, but Emma felt strangely like she was looking at a transplant in the mirror. She reached her hand forward and pretended she was an alien. That made it a little more bearable.

She moved over to her desk covered with piles of scribbled paper, crumpled notes, and a GlassTop™ open to a thirteen page-long document. Emma had less than a few hours to go to figure out how she would conclude the single most important moment in her life, save for the time she had successfully beaten Trevor in an arm wrestling contest in front of all of his idiotic friends. She shuddered at the thought of having to give this speech in this dress, but comforted herself with the knowledge that it would be the last time she would ever have to deal with the Queen's demands. Once she became King, she would be the most powerful Royal in the entire country, perhaps even the world.

She was snapped out of her thoughts once more by another, more tentative knock at the door.

At this rate she would never finish the speech. She said a curt "Come in!" expecting Bishop or Donna, but to her surprise, it was Vera. Emma's heart beat just a little bit faster, and she stood up immediately.

"Oh! Hello!" she screeched as normally as she could.

"Hi," Vera said softly. She held out four pairs of pain-inducing shoes. "The Queen sent me to equip you with the best shoes for tonight." She looked Emma up and down, and Emma became painfully aware of her discomfort in this dress. "You look . . . different."

"Different, good?" Emma asked.

"Different," Vera said decidedly. She placed the shoes on the floor, and smiled briefly at Emma. Vera had stunningly red hair and the kind of face that reminded you of a mime, in a good way.

"Anyways, I guess I'll see you tonight," Vera said abruptly after silence had stretched between them for quite some time.

"Don't you want to see which ones I choose?" Emma asked, aware that her voice was spiking a little bit desperately. Vera merely smiled, and moved toward the door.

"See you tonight, Princess."

With the soft clink of the door behind her, Vera was gone back into the mysterious world of Royal Maid work that Emma had never really been able to understand. Ever since that blurry night at SuperBowl Ball under one of the many staircases in the Castle, nothing had been the same between them. Emma stood for a few moments in contemplative silence, relishing Vera's lavender essence and the exciting flurry in the pit of her stomach. When Brandy meowed loudly, Emma jerked her head around to see her tabby cat and only ally spread across the bed in utter luxury.

"You're right, Brandy. When I'm King it will all change."

"Why would anyone want to give up being a princess?" asked the familiar high-strung voice from behind her. Queen Donna strolled in through Emma's door, eying Emma's outfit suspiciously.

"Because it is an outdated, entirely sexist, downright idiotic title," Emma responded. "What, are you sending the whole Castle to check in on me?"

"I just wanted to make sure everything was going according to plan in here," Queen Donna said stiffly. "And trust me, becoming King won't make the Royalty any less sexist." She was dressed in her absolute finest—a sequin-studded floor length gown that hugged her curvy figure tightly. Her blonde curled bob was pinned on top of her head in an elegant bird's nest.

"How is *that* supposed to be Martha Washington?" Emma asked with a scoff. Queen Donna pointed to her embroidered hair clip, which read "Martha" in bold letters.

"Sexy Martha Washington," Donna corrected her.

"You know, I can't believe that you buy into that," Emma said. "It's a ridiculously archaic—"

"Tradition that only reinforces the patriarchal

structure of the American Royalty, which continues to disenfranchise those who are not white, and male," Donna finished for her. Emma stared at Donna, dumbfounded.

"I read your Chatters," Donna said. "But what you're missing is that you have to play the game in order to win."

Emma looked at herself in the mirror and realized that standing next to her gloriously elegant stepmother, she looked like a disheveled ghost who had recently gotten in a fight. She saw Donna's eyebrows rise and knew what she was going to say next.

"You know, it wouldn't kill you to put some effort into your appearance. Maybe some make-up, or something with your hair," Donna said.

"You never know, my *Queen*," Emma drawled sarcastically. "What if I tripped and fell onto a curling iron and tragically cut my days far too short? Then you would probably regret that advice, huh?"

Donna crossed the room and pushed Brandy off of the bed without pause. "This is not a joke, you know. If you want to be successful in this world, you have to present yourself in a certain way. This could be the most important day of your life."

"Or it could be the most important day of Kyle's life," Emma said bitterly. "I swear, if my father promised to give it to *Kyle* of all people, I will just—"

"Calm down, Emma," Donna answered. "Nobody promised anybody anything."

"Exactly," Emma said. "Nobody promised me anything, either. So what's the point of all this stupid pageantry if I'm just going to go up there and watch as one of my unqualified brothers gets the crown?"

Emma jammed pair after pair of stilettos onto her feet, stumbling around for a few steps, and then ripping the shoes off in disgust as she decided against them.

"You know, you could be a little more careful with those shoes," Queen Donna said. Emma chose not to respond. Donna cleared her throat.

"Look, I just came to double-check that you

would be ready, presentable, and . . . speech-prepared," Donna said airily. Emma stopped cold in her shoe process and turned slowly to face Donna.

"What do you mean, speech-prepared?" Emma asked suspiciously.

Queen Donna shrugged. "Speech-prepared? I said ready and presentable," Donna said with a wry smile.

Emma felt her heart soar with the buoyancy of potential Kingship once more. She knew Donna was absolutely manipulating her, but nonetheless, the shining image of the angelic crown burned in her eyes. Donna stood up and walked to the door, eying Emma as she crossed the room.

"Wear the third pair," she said as she left. Emma looked after her for a moment, basking in the itching kind of irritation she always felt when she interacted with Donna. Then, her eyes landed on the stuffed sock on her desk, the very same one she had stolen from Trevor earlier that morning in order to mess with him as much as possible. She went over to the sock and slowly withdrew a bag of very stinky weed. She sniffed it with mild interest. She had never smoked weed before, because she knew she could not give anyone any reason to stop her from becoming King. But holding the weed in her hands, she felt a strange urge to find out what this thing was all about. Then Brandy meowed loudly, and Emma jumped.

"You're right," Emma said resolutely. "Absolutely right." She held the sock in her hand and had a much better idea. She looked down at her GlassPhone™ and smiled. She knew what she could do to ensure that her younger half-brother did not make it to the throne.

She charged out into the hallway in a rush and almost ran directly into a wall of bustling servers. There were caterers, event planners, flower boys, and more—all doing their best to find their way to the outer gardens. But no Freemason had ever built a castle in a sensible manner, and no hired help could ever find their way. This nonsensical layout had turned out to be a blessing to the Royal children. They grew up in its labyrinth, and knew how to take advantage of each and every secret passage for their own personal bidding. Emma, for example, knew the best way to gain entry into each of her brother's rooms through the trap doors hidden in their bathrooms and closets that could only be opened by digging her family Square and Compass ring into a tiny keyhole. So, she darted through the throngs of workers, turned left at the marble busts of the Founding Fathers, turned right at the portrait of George Washington being crowned King, and headed straight through the stable passageway. She opened the closet, climbed up into the attic, crawled through the air duct for seven minutes making sure to take the right fork after the possum skeleton, and finally deposited herself with a thud in Kyle's closet.

Her heart pounded madly even though she had done this many times before. She tentatively opened the closet door and emerged into his oppressively damp room. There, on the bed in front of her, was the softly sleeping form of Kyle. From the looks of it, he had been crying, or maybe he had fainted—which was how his pale frame usually looked. She watched his pretty face for a moment; it was rarely this relaxed. Then, she tiptoed around him to his bedside table, opened his phone, and pulled up RoyalChatterStream. She smiled devilishly and began typing as fast as her fingers could muster. When she had done her damage, she reached into her pocket and withdrew the weed from her pocket. She placed it delicately on his bedside table, and snapped a picture, sending it straight to the Stream. She turned around to tiptoe back, but a familiar red-headed face caused her to emit a very strangled yelp.

Standing in the corner was Bishop, eyes wide. He waved a solemn hello to Emma, and Emma waved back. She retreated back into the air duct trapdoor, confident that she had escaped unscathed. Bishop had never told a Royal secret to anybody, and she didn't see why he would start now. She snaked back through the Castle hallways with a bouncier step and a brighter smile, because it was about time things happened her way, for once. She barged through the Castle hallways wishing she could be on roller skates, and proceeded to the Kingly Passage, which usually depressed her due to its stuffiness.

But this time, as she walked past the portrait of Washingtonian rulers, she imagined herself hanging up next to them. Next to the much younger and skinnier portrait of her father was an empty frame reserved for the soon-to-be-announced King. She smiled at the thought of a woman next to all these old dudes, and wondered just how many times Washington would roll over in his grave thanks to her. The thought gave her the kind of fluttering deep in the pit of her stomach that she imagined skydivers or people in love felt. Then the fluttering started to gurgle a little, and she clutched her stomach in surprise. She never knew nerves could feel this real.

She continued down the corridor to find the frenzied gatekeeper who controlled all passage in and out of her father's realm, Lorena.

"Hi," Emma said after a few moments passed and Lorena did not look up from her manic typing.

"He's busy," came Lorena's curt reply.

"It's urgent," Emma responded, and the growing madness in the pit of her stomach seemed to agree with the urgency.

"I'm sorry, but he simply cannot be interrupted."

King Jonathan yelled from inside the room, "Lorena! Do we have any more cinnamon buns?"

Emma and Lorena stared each other down. Emma narrowed her eyes. Lorena matched her narrowed eyes, and raised her an eyebrow raise. Then, Emma lunged to the door. Lorena jumped to her feet to block her, but was just a few moments too late.

"Dad, we need to talk!" Emma shouted as she burst through the door.

"I'm sorry, sir, I did my best to stop her!" Lorena screeched.

Both women stood in the doorway, staring at the King of the United States of America lounging on the floor in his underwear, building a puzzle and covered in sticky cinnamon bun sugar. Emma barreled forward.

"Dad, I know this is a really hard decision to make and there are a lot of factors that go into it but the fact remains that I am the best candidate for King," Emma breathed out in a huff. The urgency in the pit of her stomach had started to make her feel more than a little in danger. "I'm the smartest, I'm the most experienced, I'm the most successful, really, I'm the best and only choice for King, and I just think you need to know that."

King Jonathan stared back at Emma, and she felt as if her gut was going to burst out of her body.

"Okay," he said simply.

"Okay?" Emma asked. "You mean it?"

King Jonathan did not have time to respond, because then Emma quite literally felt her gut bursting. The confusing mixture of warmth spread down her body and the knowledge that she had just soiled the only gown that wasn't entirely hideous came as an afterthought. Right now, the only thing that mattered was the feeling of warm liquid flowing down her leg.

"I have to go!" she shouted, and sprinted out of the room. She struggled to walk to her room with her backside pressed firmly against the wall, which proved to be challenging considering the vast magnitude of party-related frenzy. Maybe she was going to reign over the country, but first she had to establish rule over her own bowel movements.

CHAPTER FIVE

Trevor awoke to the consistent buzzing of his phone, which appeared to him as a growling coyote in his dream-induced fugue state. So, he reached out his fist and smashed the coyote's snapping snout as hard as he could. Only when he felt splinters of glass in his hand did he realize that he had smashed another GlassPhone™. He groaned and rubbed his eyes, struggling to withdraw his mind from the depths of weed-induced sleep. He had indeed found his emergency stash of weed, hidden stealthily behind the leather-framed Royal portrait of himself proudly displayed in his room next to his mirror. He rolled out of his leather-covered bed, and grimaced as his sweaty skin stuck to the leathered blanket. Before Trevor could even figure out what time it was, Bishop appeared with a new phone in hand.

"New phone, sir?"

"Thanks, Bishop," Trevor murmured.

"There was an updated model six minutes ago," Bishop said. Trevor accepted the phone groggily.

"What time is it?"

"11:42 in the morning, sir."

"That's all?" Trevor exclaimed. "I thought it had been hours!"

"It has only been twenty-five minutes, sir," Bishop answered.

Trevor sank back onto his bed with hunched shoulders and a distinct lack of a grasp on time. When his brand new GlassPhone™ buzzed once more, he looked down and saw that he had no fewer than twenty-four Direct Chatters from a variety of Dukes and Duchesses.

@DukeTommyMadisonOfficial: Dude. Tough break. Better luck with the whole King thing next time.

@THEDuchessSardine: You fell asleep so I left to go get more iced coffee. BTW Kyle is going to be King, but just said some weird shit too.

@LorettaBeretta: Hah! So much for your wonderful future as the King of the World, huh? BTW I miss u

Trevor felt ill, and it wasn't just the overwhelming body heat due to napping under a leather blanket. A message from his ex, Loretta, could only mean that something incredibly awesome or awful had happened to him—and from the tone, this seemed to land on the awful side of things. He clutched his stomach, and wondered if he had accidentally eaten a laxative cookie. He felt like a pile of worms were climbing over each other in the pit of his stomach and fighting to see who could make him vomit first. Was this what the peasants called "anxiety"?

"What happened, Bishop?" Trevor asked with trepidation. In response, Bishop clapped to turn on the GlassTV™. There was Jane, once again, in a mass of screaming fans outside the wall to the Royal Village.

"Jane," Trevor murmured under his breath.

"That's right, we are here on the ground floor of the Royal Village wall, and we have some *radical* statements from Prince Kyle on RoyalChatterStream," Jane said. A stream of Chatters flashed across the screen.

> **@PRINCEKYLE:** I really do not actually care about any of the charities I supported and I just did it cuz I thought it would make me look good...haha fooled you all!

> **@PRINCEKYLE:** How do you know if you poop too much? Cuz I think I poop a lot!

> **@PRINCEKYLE:** I think that Canada is better than America, and I love maple syrup more than apple pie!

@PRINCEKYLE: I love you Coach Nena!!!!!!!!!111!

@PRINCEKYLE: That last tweet was a mistake. Meant to say I love Canada again.

@PRINCEKYLE Chattered an image: Does any1 know where to find more weed?

The picture featured a bag of weed resting on Kyle's bedside table. Jane reappeared on screen, emanating profuse joy.

"Yes, that is correct, we have received images straight from the presumptive successor to the crown, displaying weed and asking the world for more," Jane said. "Despite Prince Trevor's best legalization efforts, marijuana is still an illegal substance punishable by six minutes of imprisonment in the Royal Stocks. Will the Crown punish him, or will the Royalty slip by the law once more? Thoughts from Prince Kyle supporters?"

She turned to a middle-aged peasant wearing an "I <3 King Kyle" shirt next to him.

"How does this affect your thoughts of Prince Kyle's ability to be King?" Jane asked.

The woman looked into camera and screamed, "I *love* Prince Kyle!" She then shrilly screeched a high-pitched tone for forty-five seconds straight.

"There you have it, folks," Jane said.

Trevor clapped his hands to turn the GlassTV™ off. He had heard enough. Emma had most certainly been the cause. He had to keep his eyes open; she could be lurking around any corner, digital or otherwise. He had to be more discerning with his naps. He had always thought if anyone were to beat him in the race to the crown, it would be Emma of all people. *She* was at least a worthy opponent. But Kyle? Really? Kyle? That guy wet his bed until he was twelve years old. Well, actually a few years earlier, but Trevor had taken it upon himself to pee on Kyle's bed in the middle of each night.

Trevor lurched to his feet once more, throwing on his sticky leather bathrobe and charging out the door toward the Kingly Passage. There was only one person who could make the worms in his stomach stop what they were doing. He barreled past the frenzy of workers, not even caring if they saw some of his downstairs when the wind flapped through the robe. He charged past the line of Washingtons on the wall, entered the Octagonal Office, and smiled the smile that always worked.

"Hi, Lor," Trevor said with a soft smile. "How're the cats?"

Lorena laughed heartily. "They're driving me crazy, as usual. Big day today, huh?"

Trevor groaned and fluttered his eyes in the calculated way that seemed to always make people forget what they were talking about.

"You're telling me!" His eyes darted to his father's ornate door. "Hey, I don't suppose my father is free now, is he?"

Lorena grimaced. "Oh, sorry, Trevor, but he made it very clear he was not to be disturbed."

Trevor nodded and leaned over her desk ever so

slightly. "Are you sure?" As Trevor leaned, his belly hit a framed picture of Lorena's cats on her desk and made it wobble. Lorena's smile dropped just a few degrees.

"Yes, I'm sorry, Trevor."

Trevor leaned in even closer and smiled. "It's just that I really need his opinion on, like, six different pairs of shoes for tonight, and it's kind of urgent."

The picture frame fell to the desk with a clatter, and Lorena's smile dropped even lower. Trevor could feel that he was losing her, and he did his best to funnel every ounce of charm he could muster into his broad smile. Unfortunately, his breath still reeked from his recent weed usage and he could not remember the last time he had truly brushed his teeth.

Lorena stared at Trevor, and Trevor stared back, and then at the same time they both lurched toward the door. Trevor reached the handle just a moment earlier and yanked it open as fast as he could. The King was lying down on his back, mostly naked and as portly as ever. Mounds and mounds of candy wrappers surrounded him and the sickeningly sweet smell of cinnamon glaze wafted up from his bulging body. Trevor would have grimaced if he hadn't seen this sight many times before.

"Hi, Trevor," Jonathan said without looking up.

"Did you really tell Kyle he could be King?! I mean, Emma I can understand, but Kyle? Are we thinking of the same Kyle?" Trevor screeched.

"I'm sorry, sir," Lorena began from the doorway, "but he just barged past me. Your children don't really have good manners!"

King Jonathan held up his hand and silenced the both of them. He nodded for Lorena to leave, and motioned for Trevor to sit down. Trevor made his way to the stately couch in the corner and perched in his bathrobe, his nether regions on full display.

"This is not how it is going to go down," Trevor said forcefully. "This is my birthright. I have been first in line my whole life, and what the hell has

Kyle done? Some humanitarian bullshit? I'm the real ruler. I'm the real Washington. I'm the real artist. I'm the real King."

King Jonathan slowly sat up, perching on his elbows. He resembled a beached whale that was slowly and painfully dying. As he wheezed and looked Trevor in the eye, Trevor wondered if this was what he would look like in his own decrepit old age. The thought made him want to vomit, so he kept talking to stop himself.

"Plus with that whole weed picture, I mean, come on! You have to know that you can't Chatter stuff like that, you just have to! Have I ever been caught with anything like that? Okay, yes, maybe like three or fourteen times but I served my six minutes in the Royal Stocks and paid the price!" Trevor burbled. He felt a wave of unruly emotion rise up within him, and he fell to his feet. Before he knew what was happening, hot moisture rapidly flooded down his face.

"I want to be King so badly! Please, Dad, please!"

Trevor said as he loudly wept. His shoulders shook with rapid sobs for far too long. The shame, humiliation, and moisture overwhelmed him entirely.

"Okay," King Jonathan finally said. "You can be King."

"I can?" Trevor asked.

"Yes. You can be King. Just don't tell any of your siblings."

"Okay," Trevor said slowly, rising to his feet. "Okay! Yes. Of course! Thank you, thank you!" He ran to his Dad and hugged him, trying to pick him up in the process but struggling between the mutual girths of their two stomachs. He settled for a strong pat on the back, and then turned to leave.

"Remember to be on time to the Queen's family meeting!" King Jonathan called after him.

"Yeah, okay!" Trevor called back, already forgetting what his father had just said. He bounded out of the room, cheerily shouted a goodbye to the disgruntled Lorena, and decided that this was time for a celebration. After all, you were only told you were going to be King once in your life, and twenty-six times in your dreams. He skirted past the bustling workers in the ornate maze of hallways, and headed toward his favorite place in this whole village. He paused for a moment outside of the secret passage, briefly considering going back to his room for some clothes, and then shrugged. He was going to be King; he could do whatever he wanted. So he pressed his ring to the tiny keyhole behind the portrait of The Crossing of Delaware and went to celebrate.

CHAPTER SIX

"**A**nd so then, I said, 'Dear Father, I'm going to be King. Whether you like it or not.' And do you know what he did?" Trevor asked to the sea of watchful faces before him. They waited with baited breath.

"Well, I'll tell you what he did. He said, 'You *are* going to be King, son.'" With that, everyone erupted into ecstatic cheers. Trevor was in his favorite bar, the Green Dragon Tavern. It was an underground and incredibly secretive affair that catered exclusively to the Royal elite. The bar was modeled in the likeness of a speakeasy, because it actually had been one during the 1940 Royal Prohibition, when King Lawrence George Washington had drank too much wine at a Christmas party and declared alcohol illegal for two days in the Royal Village. It had been a trying time for all Royals involved, and it had taken two days of intense lobbying from the Royal youth for King Lawrence to realize the horrific mistake he had made.

Princess Hallie, the most vibrant Princess ever to grace the American Royalty, had personally seen to the construction of the bar during prohibition. Although Princess Hallie tragically died in a mysterious biking accident at age twenty-seven, her legacy still lived on, in the very literal bust of her that stood in the center of the room. It was rumored that in the toughest of times, if you whispered your troubles to Princess Hallie, she would give you the answers that you needed. To this day, the bust still radiates a warm, peaceful heat that seems reminiscent of Princess Hallie's combustible spirit.

The bar was darkly lit and filled with old, dusty tables and rickety chairs. Candles cast romantic shadows across the walls that only made Trevor's story seem that much more impressive. He was surrounded by some of his closest "friends," in the very loose Royal sense of the word. Duchess Sardine Burr sat next to him, her eighth iced coffee of the day firmly in her grasp. She clung to his side because that was the only space in which she wouldn't be openly mocked and ridiculed by the rest of the Royals around her. Duke Tommy Madison, the idealistic and pudgy young Royal newly entering the social scene hung onto every word Trevor said with rapt attention. Duke Thurston Adams, an older cousin who was more "respectable," but still a child at heart, drank his sixth scotch of the early afternoon and swayed a bit in his seat. Duke Oscar Jay, the forgotten descendant of the forgotten John Jay, sat in the corner because he was always a bit too nervous to sit too close to the more important Royalty. Finally, Duke Tristan Hamilton rounded out the scene—Trevor had never really enjoyed the competition he brought, but understood that having such a handsome man in his crew would make him seem that much more desirable as a leader.

Trevor smiled in satisfaction as he saw his friends, family, and lovers absorbing the news that their bar buddy would be the most powerful man in the world in a few hours' time. He sipped his Madeira wine and reveled in the elation of undivided attention.

"Hey, when's that album coming out?" Tommy Madison asked earnestly. Trevor smiled broadly.

"I'm glad you asked, Tommy," Trevor responded. "I've been laying down some *sick* beats, and I think it could be ready any day now."

"I thought Kyle was going to be named King," Tristan said. "I heard him say it himself."

Trevor rolled his eyes widely, and fired off a glare toward Tristan.

"That's exactly what we want you to think, Tristan," Trevor said wisely.

"It is?" he asked gullibly, his shark-tooth necklace glistening against his tanned and uncomfortably thick neck.

"How else is the party tonight going to have any surprises?" Trevor asked.

"Oh, I see," Tristan said amiably. Trevor kept Tristan around because he was as easy to control as an inbred Golden Retriever.

"I think you'll be a great King!" Oscar Jay said from the corner.

"Nobody asked you," Thurston said in the softly biting tone that his sixth scotch always brought out. The rest of the group laughed, and Trevor smiled with the buoyant energy of whiskey-induced joy and his own self-belief. He was a great leader for this social crew, so he could only imagine he would be a fantastic leader for the rest of the country. Imagine the epic parties he would throw, and the spectacular joy he would spread across the land! They would sing drunken bar songs of him for ages.

Sardine brought over shots of Whiskey Rebellion for the crew, and Trevor distantly wondered if he should be drunk for the ceremony that night. Then he remembered that George Washington had been so drunk during his own coronation that he very publicly peed into Thomas Jefferson's top hat. Sardine raised her glass, and suddenly everyone was toasting to the new King of America: Trevor George Washington. He smiled, clinked his glass to theirs, and downed the mixture of caustic alcohol. His giddiness grew the longer he repeated the phrase over and over in his head: King Trevor George Washington.

He lurched to his feet; almost spilling Sardine's drink in the process, and gestured to the bartender.

"Another round, barkeep! We've got all the time in the world!"

In fact, they did not, but Trevor did not care—now that he was basically King, he could do whatever he wanted and nobody could tell him otherwise.

CHAPTER SEVEN

Queen Donna stood in the shadows of the Queen's Lair, deep below the bellows of the Castle. The dusty, cobbled walls of her secret workspace were filled with maps, schemes, and plans to rule the world, complimented by the delightful scent of cinnamon candles. She reached out her hand and circled the country of Belgium in red ink. It would soon be hers.

"Here you go, m'lady," the screeching voice of Janice Hanice said from behind her. Donna turned around to see the hunchbacked librarian in all her glory. Janice Hanice, sometimes known as the

Hooded Librarian, resembled the sort of woman one would find lurking on a street corner, shouting at people who rode bikes that they should wear helmets. Despite her stooped back and aggressively wrinkled face, Janice Hanice's rule of the Royal Archives meant that she had access to each and every document, dating back to the Constitution itself. Speaking of which, Janice pulled out the twelfth page of the Constitution from behind her back and presented it to Donna. Donna examined the gnarled page carefully.

"I don't see it," she said flatly. Janice produced a magnifying glass, which Donna peered through and finally made out the very tiny, very tight script in the corner of the bottom of the corner in the back. As Donna slowly read, she began to smile. This was exactly what she needed.

"Thank you, that'll be all Janice Hanice," Donna said curtly.

"Of course m'lady, of course," Janice Hanice said, and left the lair walking backwards and bowing. Donna exhaled in glory—this was her sure-fire path to success and domination. This was her key to placing the Royal fools around her where they needed to be, so that she could craft the world in *her* image. It was what she envisioned every night as she tried to fall asleep amidst King Jonathan's rampant snoring.

"Are you sure that'll actually work?" asked a voice from the deeper part of the shadows. Donna jumped.

"I told you not to do that down here," Donna said. "Sneaking around the air ducts is one thing, but please, give my lair some respect."

"Do I scare you?" Lexington Adams asked. Donna looked back at him and laughed. The last thing he could do was scare her. She eyed him closely and once again felt like she wanted to kiss him, slap him, or both. Lexington was a short munchkin of a Royal descendant—the Adams line seemed to shrink an inch or two every generation, leaving Lexington a very adorable five-foot-four.

He had the kind of dark eyes that suggested he was always hiding something, and he usually was. He was such a nefarious schemer that King Jonathan had banished Lexington from the Royal Village on the eve of his wedding to Donna. Lexington had conspired to sabotage Jonathan and Donna's wedding, and he had very nearly succeeded. Donna had always claimed innocence in the entire scandal and publicly denounced Lexington as a lovesick, unstable man. But the public did not know that Donna had been meeting with Lexington secretly for years, and that she found his crazed romanticisms incredibly sexy.

It may have been many years, but Donna still felt a surge of passion when she looked at Lexington, one that Jonathan just did not inspire. At the same time, she knew that there would come a day when she would have to sacrifice this man for her own good. She would do that effortlessly.

"No, you don't scare me," Donna answered flatly, when Lexington seemed like he still wanted an answer to his very obvious question. "And yes, I am sure this will work. Men are so much easier to control than anyone likes to admit."

"Including me?" Lexington asked.

"Especially you."

Donna looked over at the clock. The family meeting was a mere sixteen minutes away and she knew without a doubt that nobody from the family would be there. Yes, she had planned for that, but it didn't stop it from annoying the hell out of her.

"These damn kids can never be on time for *anything*," she said.

"I don't see why you don't just let them destroy themselves," Lexington said.

"Because that's far less satisfying," Donna answered. "And because we have the tools to take them all down at once, King Jonathan included, and not just in the public humiliation kind of way."

The shrill ring of Donna's GlassTV™ interrupted the evil scheming, and much to her annoyance she found one of her least favorite faces in the world: Jane.

Lexington said, "Jane? That reporter who you tried to—"

"Be quiet," Queen Donna said, cutting off Lexington abruptly. "You have to leave."

"What?"

"You have to leave. Now. Go through the portrait door and get out of here."

"Why?" Lexington asked as he peeled back the portrait of Martha and prepared to trek through the underground. Queen Donna wheeled around to face Lexington, a cool aggression settling in her heart.

"She's close."

She passionately kissed Lexington and then shut the portrait on him without another word. There were many more important things to focus on, like whether or not the call was coming from inside the Castle. The shrill ring of her GlassTV™ sounded out once more, this time with the face of DeMarcus Nephews, the wisest publicist alive. He was fifty-six and had probably been that exact age for his entire life. His striking contrast of dark chocolate skin and snow-white teeth enabled him to operate with a stoicism that demanded complete obedience. He had spent his younger years working for pop stars and was single-handedly responsible for launching Augustus into international stardom at the tender age of four. Queen Donna trusted him like a hired assassin—he would get the job done, no matter the cost to anyone who got in the way. Queen Donna reflexively fixed her hair and answered the call.

"Hi, DeMarcus," she said.

"Listen, we've got three stories we need to stay on top of today," DeMarcus said.

"Lay it on me," she responded.

"Kyle," DeMarcus said gruffly. Donna nodded. "There's now a ChatterStream drug scandal."

Donna groaned. She had dealt with this with Trevor far too many times already.

"I've released a statement saying the photo was doctored," DeMarcus said. "But I suggest you handle it internally." Donna would ensure that Kyle did not have any further opportunities to derail her plans.

"Next up: Trevor's drunken bathrobe rampage," DeMarcus said. Donna felt the familiar bile rising in her throat.

"You mean that naked sprint this morning?" Donna asked.

"No. Another one." DeMarcus shared the shaky video footage of Trevor in the Green Dragon Tavern, that seedy little place that the Royal children liked to go to drink and do weird things with each other in the dark. Trevor stood on top of a table, leading a round of "I Just Can't Wait To Be King," from the Disney classic "The Lion King: A George Washington Allegory." The country's trashiest Royal youth, including that insufferable Duchess Sardine Burr, surrounded him. Donna watched the video wordlessly. She should have married Trevor off to Germany when she had the chance. He could have used some of Princess Adelaidesternness.

When Trevor finished the song, he took another

long, deep swig from the bottle of Madeira he was holding onto for dear life, and looked directly in the camera. "I'm going to be King!" he shouted with a wide, drunken grin. Then, of course, he took off his leather robe and swung it around his head while everyone around him cheered loudly. He leaned over and tried to make out with Duchess Sardine. She firmly swatted him away, and he tripped and fell onto the ground.

When the video was over, DeMarcus's face reappeared, emblazoned with the same somber expression.

"ChatterStream is calling it #BathrobeGate," DeMarcus said. Ever since the 1972 Broken Gate Scandal at the Royal Stables during the annual Royal Horse Golf Tournament, the media seemed to love ending any scandal with "-Gate." Donna thought it communicated a clear lack of imagination.

"Where is he now?" Donna asked.

"I sent some people to bring him home and sober him up," DeMarcus answered.

"What's the third problem?" Donna asked, her mind racing through the litany of possibilities. There was the Lexington Adams situation, her husband's inability to do anything besides eat cinnamon buns, Emma's secret, Trevor's secret, Kyle's secret, her own secret, the Great Fake Washington Secret . . . The list went on and on.

DeMarcus shared another video, this one featuring a plain, yet oddly comfortable man standing on stage in front of a large group of people. He appeared to be leading some sort of conference, or perhaps a dance routine. She could not imagine why else there would be this many people watching this peasant man. He stood in front of a sign that read "Kennedy: The Change We Need."

The plain man opened his mouth and began to speak. Donna was immediately bored by the lack of theatrics in his voice, but she struggled to listen.

"This country is being 'run' by a group of rich

outdated, removed socialites who can't even look up from their own idiocy long enough to care about the people of this fine nation!" His passionate speech was met with sparse, albeit enthusiastic, applause. "Do you know that they gather, and they dress up as *Sexy Slaves* at their fancy parties that our tax money funds? Do you know that they use our money to fund their schools, their hospitals, and their communities—while we get their discarded leftovers? We need to end this. We need change!" This was met with a round of raucous applause once more. Donna had spaced out at some point during the first sentence, as she had far more important things to occupy her brain. DeMarcus reappeared, and Donna looked back at him blankly.

"A scrappy new politician named Kennedy is trying to mobilize a movement to overthrow the Royal family," DeMarcus summarized. Donna laughed out loud.

"That's preposterous," she scoffed.

"It is something we need to keep an eye on,"

DeMarcus responded. "His great-uncle was some sort of activist back in the '50s."

"Never heard of him," Donna said.

"He's the senator that intervened in the Peruvian Coffee Crisis and stopped World War X after thirty minutes," DeMarcus said. Donna shrugged; it sounded vaguely familiar.

"Just something we need to be aware of, especially as the entire world tunes in tonight," DeMarcus said sternly. Donna sighed heavily. Keeping this Royal family together, presentable, and alive had been one of the hardest struggles of her entire life. They would never know what lengths she went to in order to keep them protected and functioning. They would never know that she was the one who bailed Trevor out of jail, erased Emma's failing grade from her Yale record, or kept the restraining orders filed against Kyle quiet. They would never know what she had sacrificed for them, and she wasn't even their real mother. But soon enough, it would be Donna's time. Soon enough, the selfish children and clueless husband would be forced to step aside, and give her the respect she deserved.

"Your Highness?" DeMarcus asked, snapping Donna out of her revelry.

"Yes, DeMarcus?"

"There is one more thing," he said. "That reporter Jane."

"Jane," Donna muttered under her breath with hatred. There was nothing she detested more than nuisances, and Jane was the noisiest nuisance of them all. "She called me just before you did."

DeMarcus narrowed his eyes. "Be careful. We've seen her snooping around the Royal Gate all day."

"There's no way she can get inside," Queen Donna snapped, although realistically she knew that there were more entrances to this place than even she could possibly know. DeMarcus remained stone-faced.

"Just keep an eye out."

Donna nodded and turned off the communication with a quick clap. She looked once more at her clock and saw that the afternoon meeting loomed ever closer. Soon, she would be able to tackle the issues that really mattered, like Belgium.

"Belgium," she muttered under her breath, turning once more to face her map of the world. She stared at the circled country on her map, and then decided it was time to make sure the family did not ruin her destiny as a Franklin to win back the land that was rightfully hers.

First on her list was Kyle. She needed to make sure the sack of sadness known as the youngest child would not run off the rails she had so painstakingly set down for him. She marched through the hallways to Kyle's room, and opened the door to find the shades drawn with Kyle facedown on his pillow. His disheveled black hair and sweaty workout clothes suggested that he had not even showered since the gym-fainting incident. She stood over him and stared down at him for a few long moments. She wondered what his parents had done wrong, and shook him roughly.

"Ow!" he exclaimed as he groggily rolled over.

"Get up," she said.

"Mom?" he asked sleepily.

"No," Queen Donna said abruptly. "It's your Queen."

Kyle slowly rolled over to peer up at his stepmother, and Donna unflinchingly stared back. She saw the bag of weed on his bedside table and her anger grew.

"You know that you could get thrown in the Royal Stocks for this," Donna said.

"What?" Kyle asked, his eyes focusing on the bag. "Th-th-that's not mine!"

"And you know if you're in the Royal Stocks tonight, that doesn't look good for your Kingship chances," Donna said.

"I swear! I didn't do it!"

The look on Kyle's face, and the self-evident knowledge that Kyle would rather cut off a limb than get in trouble made her remember that this was not a child who would go against her wishes. It was at that point that Donna thought back to the conversation with Emma, and smelled the scheming of another all over this room. Maybe Emma was a far worthier opponent than she had given her credit for. But, she was way too deep into her scolding to back out now. There was only one course she could chart: full-speed ahead. In fact, maybe even ramp it up a bit.

"You're a disgrace to the entire Washington line!" Donna shouted. "I can't believe we call you a Prince. Do you know what this is going to do to your father?!"

"I didn't do anything!" Kyle shouted back. "All I wanted to do was exercise!"

"You need to get out of your drug den, get dressed, and get your ass to the family meeting, okay?"

"Okay," Kyle responded meekly. She stood up, pleased with her intimidating prowess, and stared at Kyle's pale complexion. "And dear God, please, put some spray tan on or something."

She turned to walk away, and as she opened the door, she found a caterer standing directly outside.

"Sorry," the caterer mumbled, and began to walk away quickly. Donna sensed something was not right.

"Wait!" Donna shouted. "Come back here," she ordered. Slowly, the caterer moved back toward Donna. She was essentially swimming in clothes that seemed at least five sizes too big for her. She cast her eyes down at the floor and would not look up.

"Look at me," Donna ordered once more. With seemingly no other choice, the caterer lifted her eyes up to make eye contact with Donna. Donna gasped.

"Jane," she murmured with hatred.

"Donna," Jane said calmly. "Nice to see you again."

"It's Queen Donna," Donna said. "What the hell are you doing here?"

Jane smiled, gesturing to Kyle's closed door. "Oh, you know, just getting as much background information on the 'future King' as possible."

Donna wondered just how much Jane had heard, and just how long she had been in the castle. Donna prided herself on her pristine public image, and she did not need a rant at her stepchild to surface now.

"Well, what you are doing is illegal and you need to leave," Donna said with a thinly-masked edge in her voice.

"I was just on my way out," Jane answered. Her eyes blazed as she looked Donna directly in the eye, and smiled.

"See you in a few hours," Jane said, before turning and walking away. Donna had to resist the urge to chase after Jane, because if there was one thing she hated most, it was people walking away from her. She shook her head, and returned to the more important matter at hand: conquering the party, and then Belgium, and then the world.

CHAPTER EIGHT

King Jonathan George Washington sought solace beneath the vine and fig trees in the far corners of the Royal Fields, where even the GlassPhone™ reception struggled to reach. He tried to imagine his ancestors sitting there before him. George Washington solved a multitude of problems beneath his vine and fig trees, and for years, Washingtons had retreated to the sacred spot when they needed to figure out their paths. That had been King Jonathan's grand intention, but instead, he was scrolling through RoyalChatterStream and could not stop.

@HowNowCow2: Now Trevor says he's going to be king?? WTF??

@juniperbranchhh: Kyle is idiot, at least Trev is smart.

@RoyalFever333: What do u mean? Trev can barely read!1!

Finally, hidden amidst the speculation, was the username he would recognize anywhere.

@JonathanLuvr452: King Jon is hot.

There it was. Somewhere out there, @JonathanLuvr452 truly loved him, and he truly loved him/her. Maybe he should just run away tonight, before anyone could notice he was gone. He would take his trusty steed Buttercup XVIII and live with @JonathanLuvr452 without any of this stress. He could assume a peasant identity and work as a tour guide in a rustic old town, or as a sales clerk in a Radio Shack. He hovered over @JonathanLuvr452's username, preparing himself to make the first Direct Chatter and propose the plan. But then a fig fell directly onto his head, and he looked up in dismay. That *must* have been a sign—he wasn't sure of what, but it didn't seem promising. Then he heard a shrill whistle and knew exactly what the fig signified.

Uncle Rustbatham emerged from the woods; his tawny Osprey named Scarlett perched delicately on his shoulder. Uncle Rusty was King Jonathan's father's uncle, and he was also unfathomably insane. The eighty-seven-year-old bird-of-prey enthusiast spent his days whistling at his birds, and his nights also whistling at his birds. He was grizzled, absurdly thin, and perpetually sporting an eye patch even though King Jonathan was pretty sure that he did not need one. He had a habit of disappearing for weeks at a time and reappearing with a completely different appearance, pretending as if nothing had happened.

"Thinkin' 'bout the future?" Uncle Rusty screeched in a voice that sounded far too similar to his birds. Grimble the hawk hooted from the branch directly above King Jonathan's head.

"Always," King Jonathan responded. He sunk his hands into his pockets and withdrew another cinnamon bun. He offered it to Uncle Rusty. Uncle Rusty shook his head, but Scarlett screeched and flew to grab the bun in one fell swoop.

"What's on yer mind?" Uncle Rustbatham asked as Scarlett pecked through the cinnamon bun.

"I promised the crown to both Emma and Trevor, and I know it was a bad idea, but I just couldn't handle everyone asking me things all the time! And now I have no idea who to choose or what to do or how to fix it and I want to run away forever."

Uncle Rustbatham stared at King Jonathan for many moments before finally asking, "Have you ever eaten one of these figs?"

King Jonathan shook his head. Rustbatham began to walk away, but yelled back over his shoulder, "Try one!" Half of Uncle Rusty's advice was incredibly poignant and wise, and the other half was always unusably insane. It was often impossible to tell which was which until it was too late. So Jonathan shrugged, reached upwards and plucked a fig from the tree.

It was pale green, and as soft as the belly of a Royal Possum. He bit into the fig tenderly and almost gasped at the sweetness of it. The inside was a deep, vibrant red, filled with more seeds than he could count and nearly exploding with succulent juice. Before he could lose any more of the moisture that was already dribbling down his hand, he stuffed the rest of the fig into his mouth. He swallowed it whole, and as the sweetness traveled down his throat into the pit of his stomach, he began to weep.

He felt the warm, salty tears run down his face and watched as they splashed onto the ground below him. He stared into his hands, sticky with the juice of the fig. He wondered where his life had gone. He was going to *do* things as King. Important things. He had ideas, plans, and passions. He had wanted to make a difference, once. But instead, what did he have to show for his work? He had children who were each equally unfit to take on the job they were born into, a wife who spent way too much time talking to herself in the dark shadows, two ex-wives that hated his guts, and a Boston Tea Party birthday extravaganza that he didn't even want to attend.

Slowly, his sobs calmed down and he was left with the sinking feeling of emptiness. His phone dinged, and the face of Queen Donna popped up in his Stream. It was now time for the Royal meeting, but he couldn't make his feet move. So he reached up above him, grabbed another fig, and stuffed it into his mouth. He had been King for thirty-seven years and he hadn't even eaten these figs before.

Emma sat on the floor of her bathroom, reeling just a little bit. What had happened in the last few hours was vile, and should never be talked about or mentioned ever again. She still felt utterly destroyed from the whole ordeal, and wondered if anyone had seen, heard, or god forbid, smelled any signs of the travesty. The oppressive face of Donna on her GlassPhone™ had announced the family meeting a few minutes ago, but she was in no state to see anybody right now.

Trevor and those damn cookies. He was always the one who made her want to scream, cry, and maim someone all at the same time. She should have known that he would try to sabotage her, just as she was trying to sabotage Kyle. She had to get him back in a way that would tear into his core, emotionally. She knew Trevor well enough to know that he was immune to most emotional attacks, but when there was the right opportunity, it could be devastating. Once she had torn the head off of his prized teddy bear, Mr. Brownie. He had cried for weeks, and that had only been five years ago. Imagine how devastated he would be if she ripped the head off of something or someone else he cared about that much . . . someone like Duchess Sardine. Yes, Trevor's volatile best friend was the right place to strike. If she could successfully attack Trevor's most vital source of support, she could ruin him emotionally the way he had ruined her physically.

The knock at the bathroom door would have jolted her if she had any energy left, but instead, she could only feebly wonder who was coming to see her at a time like this. She imagined Vera bringing her more shoe options and sinking to her knees to care for Emma's fractured internal organs.

"Who is it?" she asked weakly.

"It's me," came the soft reply. Emma could not exactly place the voice, but the image of Vera overwhelmed her. She fixed her hair as best as she could, and tried to pull herself together while still looking appealingly vulnerable.

"Come in," Emma responded. The door slowly opened. It seemed as if the world around her was moving in slow motion, or maybe that was just the severe dehydration. She saw a sensibly-shoed foot step into the bathroom, and looked up. She would have screamed when she saw her visitor, if she had the strength. Instead, all she could do was bask in the sinking disappointment that it was not the woman she wanted to see.

"Really?" Emma asked. "Do you just knock on doors saying 'It's me,' and see where you can get in?"

Jane looked back at her with a victorious smile. She snapped a quick photo of the remnants of Emma, sprawled across the bathroom floor.

"Pretty much. You'd be surprised how often it works," Jane responded. She was dressed as a construction worker, equipped with a tool belt and a hard hat. Emma truly, truly hated Jane, and felt the fury of the injustice of it all imbue her limbs with some semblance of energy.

"You're breaking the law," Emma said. "You know peasants can't be back here."

"You're half-naked on the bathroom floor hours

before the coronation," Jane coolly replied. "What will the people think?"

"They'll think that you're a monster," Emma said weakly. Jane chuckled, and sat down next to Emma.

"Stop chuckling," Emma said. Jane looked Emma up and down.

"Listen, you're in a very vulnerable position right now. Do what I say, and this picture won't get published," Jane said. "I think we can both help each other out."

"There's no way in hell I'll ever help you," Emma said defiantly.

"We both have a common enemy, and I think we could gain a hell of a lot from joining forces," Jane said.

"Trevor," Emma murmured, as the realization dawned on her.

"Trevor," Jane muttered with equivocal hatred. Emma looked at Jane, really considered her for the first time. Jane had always been an enemy, especially considering the Chatters Jane had written that tore apart Emma's fashion sense and described in gritty detail the time she told the Prime Minister of Norway to "go trip on a chainsaw and die" after he had drunkenly asserted that she should keep her opinions to herself at parties. But, when Emma looked at Jane's enigmatically dark eyes, she could imagine how her brother could have broken her heart. She didn't feel pity, but she felt the slightest touch of softness, and maybe a hint of identification.

"I'm listening," Emma said. She still had a few hours before she became King, which was more than enough time to destroy her brother and repair her ailing bowels.

CHAPTER NINE

Kyle sat in the Royal Family Meeting Room alone, tapping his foot and checking the time. The room was in the exact core of the Castle, and thus had no windows or the slightest indication that the outside world existed. It was the sort of grandly cavernous room that could have made a great bird atrium if Kyle had only been given the chance. Instead, it featured a long, aged, wooden table. Apparently, this was the same table from George Washington's original Mount Vernon estate. But when Kyle sat at the head of the table, he did not feel any more regal. The room was devoid of decoration, in an effort to force the Royal family to actually speak to each other. It also doubled as a safe room in the event of a Royal panic, which so far had happened twenty-nine times during the launch of each World War.

Kyle felt his back spasm with the tension of sitting upright in such a viscerally wooden chair, and so he arched his body and felt a few things crack within. In the aftermath of his hazy declaration, Kyle felt as if he was moving through a slow motion nightmare. Not only did he pass out in front of the love of his life and declare that he would be the King to the entire world, he had also peed his pants in the process. Then he had awoken to a nightmare of framed RoyalChatterStream activity. At age eighteen, his life was already over. He knew there was no way Coach Nena would ever look at him again, and he was already contemplating the best ways to disappear forever and change his identity as smoothly as possible.

He glanced again at the large clock in the center of the room. He scratched his leg. He thought about calling his stepmom, and then decided better of it. He thought about calling his real Mom, but realized he didn't even know how to reach the peasant world. His cheek was still hurting from the slap, and his pride was still reeling from the thought of being forced to roast in his sadness in the Royal Dungeon.

Just when he was contemplating returning to the gym to make the afternoon Arm-Assaulting Army workout, the ornate wooden doors in the center of the room swung open. Kyle looked up to see his father, fresh from a lengthy dose of crying. Kyle cried more than enough to know a fellow crier when he saw one. For the first time, Kyle noticed just how old his father looked. His hair was graying, his body was portly beyond recognition, and his eyes were tired. Kyle wondered if that was how he would look when he was that age, and shuddered at the thought.

Hopefully science would have caught up with them by then.

"Where is everyone?" King Jonathan asked. Kyle shrugged.

"Sorry about the whole 'I'm going to be King' thing," Kyle said sheepishly. "And I don't know who wrote those things but it wasn't me."

King Jonathan sighed and sat down across from Kyle, simply shaking his head, albeit kindly. They sat in silence, and waited for the rest of the family to come.

Trevor hadn't meant to get wasted this early in the afternoon, but sometimes the best intentions go awry. Which is exactly what he tried to explain to his stepmother as she pulled him by the arm through the secret passageways underneath the Castle.

"I'm telling you, Donna, it just happened, and who am I to argue with what felt so right?" Trevor slurred. Queen Donna continued to yank his arm without a word. He was close to the end of his patience with this woman. In a few hours' time, she wouldn't even be relevant anymore, which is exactly what he would tell her right this instant.

"You know! In a few hours, you won't be . . . you won't . . . " He slurred, his mind trailing off mid-thought. When she yanked his arm especially hard around a corner, he pulled back as hard as he could. Donna toppled to the floor with a loud clatter.

"Ah, shit Donna, I'm sorry," Trevor said, slowly giggling. His giggles grew into full-bellied laughter, and soon enough he could not contain himself. Queen Donna dusted off her formal wear, grabbed his arm, and continued walking.

"Aw, come on, I really didn't mean it! I'm sorry!" Trevor said. "Really, truly, very sorry!"

They crossed the threshold into the Castle, and

the blinding light of daytime nearly knocked Trevor over. The room spun rapidly around him and his stomach was certainly not pleased.

"Donna?" Trevor said plaintively. "I don't . . . I don't . . . feel so good."

But Donna was not listening; she was yanking him through the hallways as fast as she could.

"Donna?!" Trevor said once more, a bit more urgently. But before he could voice the fact that he was going to throw up in a matter of mere minutes, or perhaps seconds, he saw the blurry image of Emma nearing them.

"Not this way," Emma said under her breath. "Jane is impersonating a construction worker up that hallway."

Trevor heard her words as if he were a million miles away, and he only vaguely grasped their meaning. When had Jane begun a construction career? Queen Donna and Emma grabbed Trevor by each arm and hauled him to his room, where he fell down instantly onto his bed. He was so glad to have stability in his life, at last. The nauseous feeling in his stomach slowly receded. He closed his eyes so that the room would stop spinning and heard the faint voices of his stepmother and half-sister at the foot of his bed.

"What do you mean, she's looking for him?" Queen Donna asked.

"She's hell-bent on getting revenge," Emma said. "We can't have her see him like this. We have to lock him up in here until he's sober."

Trevor felt terror strike him in his core. He could feel that Emma had something else planned. He tried his best to say something, anything. He knew that there was no way in hell he wanted to be locked in his bedroom if Emma said it was a good idea. But he heard their steps recede toward the door. He used every ounce of energy to turn his face to the side, just in time to see Emma wink at him as she closed the door behind them. In a few moments, the lock of the door sealed his fate. He closed his eyes and fell into a deep abyss, even as he heard the rustling sounds of someone emerging from the shadows.

CHAPTER
TEN

By the time Queen Donna was able to successfully bring herself and the sweatpants-clad Princess to the Family Meeting, it was nearing three in the afternoon and she was incredibly pissed.

"You know you have to wear something nice tonight," Donna said. "And in costume."

"Oh, it'll be in costume," Emma responded, and Donna knew from the tone of her voice that the Princess would defy her wishes once again. Donna opened the meeting room doors without another word, and walked in to find Kyle and Jonathan both softly crying while watching GlassTV™.

Jonathan was still mostly naked, and Kyle had not bothered to remove his workout clothes from earlier. He was now reeking with the stench of yogurt left out in the sun for several days. Sometimes she did not understand how these people were still alive. Both men turned to face the women of their family, sheepishly wiping away their tears and blowing their noses.

"What are you watching?" Emma asked.

"Proposal videos," Kyle answered through his soft sobs.

"Cool," Emma responded, and pulled up a chair in between them.

"Did you make me Chatter those things?" Kyle whispered.

"Of course not! But I'm looking for whoever did, and I'll show them to mess with my brother," Emma answered. Queen Donna watched Kyle nod gratefully and clasp Emma's hand. He was so utterly foolish. Donna's chosen family pulled their chairs to directly face the GlassTV™. The three of them were coexisting more peacefully than they ever had before, and it was vividly pathetic. She eyed her husband, whose face was flushed with what easily could have been hours of tears. She looked Kyle up and down, from his disheveled head of hair to his disgustingly smelly attire. She watched Emma settle in next to them, flaunting those sweatpants like she knew just how much it bothered Donna, and she absolutely did.

"Where's Trevor?" Kyle asked innocently. Emma shrugged once more, and suddenly, Donna felt very weary. All of the stress of the day, and the week, and the lifetime was starting to catch up with her. She knew that when she signed on to the Royal family this late in the game, she would have a fair amount of hassle to deal with. But she never in a million years imagined that those foolish children and that weeping man would put up this much of a fight. She needed to prepare them for the next step if she was going to have any shot at reclaiming the Belgian kingdom that was rightfully hers, but all she wanted to do was lie down. So she did.

She sunk down to the floor, and then slowly lay down on her back. She could feel the eyes of her family on her, but she closed her own and did her best to enjoy the feeling. For a few moments nobody said anything.

"Uh, honey?" Jonathan asked.

She did not respond.

"Everything alright?" he continued.

Of course everything was not all right. Did people who were all right lie down on the floor without saying anything?

"Yes," she said stoically. She felt the family members one by one turn their attention back to the GlassTV™ in front of them. Queen Donna imagined herself on the sands of the Belgian shore, basking in the sun and reveling in her well-deserved land. Maybe she even had a tropical drink of some sort in her hand, and she certainly had some sunscreen on—protecting her flawless skin was a top priority.

She heard the soft sobs of her family a few feet away, and the muffled sounds of romantic music and cheering audiences in the aforementioned engagement videos. She imagined it was the distant echo of the Belgian sea washing over her. She felt herself slowly slipping into her most restful state; partially asleep but still in control of her consciousness, and she built a beautiful ocean before her. It was cold, colder than American beaches, but it was also much classier because it was European. The sparkling blue water stretched as far as the eye could see, but her tiny parcel of beach was just hers and hers alone.

Bernard, her muscular Belgian waffle-cooker/lover was cooking waffles next to her, the kind with chocolate and whipped cream. She bit into the waffle, and the frothy cream got all over her face. But she didn't care. Bernard wiped off the cream with a soft smile. She loved the feel of his hardened hands on her face, rough from the many years of waffle flipping. He had lived a hard life, her

Bernard, and he was a tortured soul. But they had truly found happiness together on this beach, this beach that she had ripped from the Belgians without another thought. He kept his rough hand on her cheek, and then moved his whiskered face toward hers. They began to kiss, slowly at first, and then passionately. His hand slid lower, and lower, and lower—

"Queen Donna!" Kyle shrieked, viscerally pulling Donna out of her vision. She wearily opened her eyes.

"I think you'll want to see this," came Jonathan's grave voice, the kind of gravity he reserved for news of the children making terrible mistakes. But all of the conscious children were here. So that left . . .

She jumped to her feet quickly, fueled once more by the manic need to fulfill her vision. Her family stared back at her, their eyes suggesting the truth: Trevor had done something truly stupid. But how could that be possible when he was safely passed out in his bedroom?

"Let me see," she demanded curtly. Emma pressed a few buttons on her GlassPhone™, and then the story was projected on the GlassTV™ in front of them. There were six not-safe-for-work photos of Trevor in all of his half-naked and fully-passed out glory. Donna's heart slowed just a bit. She had seen worse.

"This isn't so bad," Donna said tentatively.

"Look closer," Kyle said. Donna didn't have to, because the GlassTV™ zoomed in on the pictures to show just exactly what Trevor was wearing: boxers adorned with the Canadian Flag.

"Shit," Donna cursed under her breath. Emma continued scrolling through the picture, which featured an entire hoard of Canadian paraphernalia that was on or around Trevor, including Canadian socks, a framed picture of two Mounties, and Canadian maple syrup. Donna grimaced with each and every artifact. This would cause quite the outcry among the Royals. Those maple-chugging dogsledders would see these pictures and think that they were finally friends with America, and then navigate their way into an invitation to the next few Royal functions.

"Jane," Donna muttered under her breath.

"Jane," Emma agreed.

"Jane?" Jonathan asked.

"Jane!" Kyle said.

"She's still in the building," Donna said. An unparalleled fury rose with her, the kind that only came once in a few moons but always meant the end of someone's tragically insignificant existence. As her deeply seething anger grew hotter and hotter, fueled by the frustrations of working with a family that hindered her each and every move, she locked eyes with Emma. She saw her own anger reflected in the plain face staring back at her. If there was anything she could count on her stepdaughter for, it was being ready for a confrontation.

"What are you thinking?" Emma asked, her voice dangerously matching Donna's inner fury.

"We take care of the pest problem, once and

for all," Donna responded. Emma nodded, stood up, and began to stretch out her arms. The men of the family sat bewildered in their seats, as per usual.

"What, do we have roaches?" King Jonathan asked.

CHAPTER ELEVEN

The entire family sat in their seats around the Family Meeting table and avoided eye contact. Emma had never intended matters to end like this when she had made a deal with the devil. But as deals with the devil go, she was not entirely in control of the outcome, and she could never turn down a good fight. Trevor cleared his throat loudly across the table, and Emma looked up at him, making brief eye contact. He had two swollen eyes and a busted lip. She looked away before she could feel guilty. On the other side of the table, Queen Donna was in the process of fixing her gloriously piled hair, which had been savagely yanked in the earlier fray. King Jonathan stared down at the table before him without blinking. Kyle nursed a bruised heart, both figuratively and literally, because he had indeed been punched in the chest.

"Look, I didn't . . . " Emma started to say, and then stopped herself. She knew that she could not say anything to undo the earlier brawl, no matter how much it felt like a dream. Everything had escalated so quickly; one minute she was sneaking Jane into Trevor's room, the next she was plotting with Donna to get back at Jane for a situation she had caused, and then the next she was in the blind madness of a fistfight. Trevor spit out a mixture of blood and chipped teeth onto the table. Kyle grimaced.

"She got you pretty hard, huh?" Kyle asked.

"Actually, I think that might have been from you," Trevor answered.

"Oh. Well, it was really dark," Kyle responded. It had been very dark when the family had rushed to Trevor's room as a group and dragged the drowsy Trevor out of bed. When he had learned the news, he rushed to "fight" Jane. He stumbled out into the hall and mistook Vera for Jane, nearly punching her in the face, which made Emma push Trevor back into Kyle, which made King Jonathan step in to try and stop it. That might have been the end of it, had not Trevor retaliated and accidentally hit his father in the process, which brought the Secret Service into the fray. A confusing mixture of punches, kicks, screams, and hair pulling later, the fight had ended and the Royal family was a heap of confusion and bruises.

Emma had only meant to sabotage both of her brothers and become the ruler of the free country. Was that too much to ask? She looked around at the vacant faces before her, and then dared to look at Queen Donna. Her pristine face was absolutely, stunningly calm. She looked as if she had just had a beautiful night's sleep, or a wonderful massage. Emma kicked Trevor under the table and motioned toward Donna. His face paled instantly. Kyle looked in the same direction and saw the sight that would make any Washington's heart run cold.

Queen Donna inhaled and exhaled rapidly, like a fish washed up on shore. Then, she opened her mouth.

"Dearest family," she said, in the softest and most powerful voice that had probably ever existed. "Today, I needed One. Simple. Thing. From all of you."

Emma bristled at the term "family." It seemed presumptuous. Queen Donna cleared her throat and continued. "All I wanted, all I had asked for, was for you to all be ready, in costume, and present. Not only was this a courtesy to me, your dear stepmother, it was a simple necessity due to the fact that one of you filthy idiots will be named King tonight."

Donna looked around at each of them pointedly. Nobody could hold eye contact. "Each and every one of you is an embarrassment to the Washington name. Do you know that your ancestors fought a *war* to make this possible for you? Do you know that if George Washington had not gotten his way, this country would not have even had a King, and you would all be . . . *peasants?*" She spat the last word out as if it was poison. "Can you imagine what sort of world we would live in? A country for peasants, ruled by peasants? How many Royal horses do you think you would have?"

Kyle tentatively raised his hand.

"Two?" he suggested. Emma kicked him under the table.

"At least six," Trevor said with a wry laugh.

"No!" Donna screamed. "Zero! You would have zero Royal horses! And zero normal horses! Nobody would have any horses! Horses would probably be extinct!"

Kyle reddened to a deep, beet red.

"You had one job today, and each and every one of you messed it up. Each and every one of you is a complete and utter failure. We were going to announce who the successor will be at this meeting."

Emma's heart surged at those words, and she felt her brothers both equally stiffen next to her.

"But instead," Donna continued. "I'm just going to lock you in this room until the party. Understand? You will be brought your clothes, you will get dressed here, and then you will be led by Bishop to the party. And you will *smile*."

The children sat in silence, and Emma settled uncomfortably into the feeling of being a scolded child.

"I said, 'do you understand?'" Queen Donna repeated.

"Yes, Queen Donna," they said in unison.

"Good," she said. Then Emma squirmed in her seat as Donna cleared her throat once more and directed her attention toward King Jonathan.

"And *you*," Queen Donna spat out. King Jonathan still did not look up. "I would like to speak to you in the hallway."

Wordlessly, King Jonathan rose to his feet and shuffled out the door with Queen Donna, leaving Emma and her brothers behind. When the door slowly closed, Kyle turned around anxiously.

"Do you think she's going to hurt him?" Kyle asked.

Trevor shrugged. "All I know is that she's not going to be able to talk to me like that once my album drops, and I'm crowned King."

Emma sighed as loud as she could. "You. Are. Not. A. Rapper."

This launched the children into the kind of fight that would occupy them until they were allowed to attend the party.

Meanwhile, in the hallway, Queen Donna was reeling from the giddiness of yelling at that many people at once. Her husband stared at the ground, and she grabbed his face to make him look at her.

"Here," she said, extending her hand with that

decaying piece of parchment. King Jonathan slowly accepted it.

"What is it?" he asked, turning it over in his hands.

"It's how you're going to get out of choosing a successor tonight," she answered.

CHAPTER TWELVE

The Royal Trumpeter painstakingly made his way to the top of the Northeast parapet of the Royal Castle. From here, one could see the expanse of Virginian countryside stretching before them, preserved as it had been in their forefather's era. But instead of rolling hills as far as the eye could see, ripe for settlement, snaking highways and offensive billboards littered the horizon. The guests had begun to arrive for the party, traveling across the Royal roads by limo, car, and horse. It was all about being seen and being Chattered tonight, and the Dukes and Duchesses loved it.

The trumpeter continued the treacherous climb to the top, his feet finding the foot holes that were carved many, many years ago. As his foot slipped and he grabbed onto the rough stonewall before plummeting to certain death, he wondered if maybe he should have put his Julliard Peasant education to a different use. But alas, the Royal Trumpeter was the most respected trumpeter in the nation. It didn't hurt that his father was finally proud of him and that all his friends were intimately obsessed with the lives of the Royal family. Personally, he couldn't care less about with whom Trevor was sleeping or if Emma was shorter than she looked on Stream, but his wife just couldn't get enough of that. Plus he had a young daughter who idolized Princess Emma, and now twins on the way, and he really needed this health insurance. The Royal Trumpeter just tried to keep his head down, play when he was told, and save up enough money to be able to go to Aruba one day.

He finally made it to the very top of the Northeast

parapet, a minute or so ahead of schedule. He took a few moments to absorb the view, and imagined himself two hundred years earlier, making the same climb for the Royal family. With a loud clang, the clock tower struck six-thirty. The trumpeter took in a deep breath, lifted his trumpet to his lips, and began to play the melody that was innate by now. He sounded the joyous tune of the start of a party, his chest bursting with the effort and the American pride.

———

"What the hell is that sound?" Trevor asked with his head in between his legs. He had been unable to sleep off his mid-day hangover ever since he had been forcibly withdrawn from his slumber and thrown into a full-on melee. He clutched his swollen eyes in pain.

"It's that dumbass trumpeter," Duchess Sardine responded. She wore sunglasses that were almost as big as her entire head, and they did a hell of a good job at hiding her bloodshot eyes. The two sat in the hallway leading to the party yard, but could not bring themselves to enter, not yet. Trevor was dressed in his best George Washington attire, modeling himself after the young and handsome war general. Although he knew he looked dashing in red, he would rather die than go talk to anyone out there about his Canadian underwear exposé.

"He sounds terrible," Trevor responded. "Tell him to stop."

"I can't just tell the Royal Trumpeter to stop," Sardine said without much interest. Trevor groaned loudly.

"Then what can you do?" he asked. Sardine took a sip of her iced coffee, which was probably spiked with something. She thought for a few moments, and then shrugged. Trevor groaned once more. While Sardine had kept him company through his lowest of lows, like this moment right now, she had also proved herself to be not much of a support system when he needed her. He put his head back down between his knees and took deep breaths, focusing on making himself feel better. This proved to be harder than he thought.

"I think I'm going to be sick," he murmured under his breath. Sardine was busy on her GlassPhone™, laughing at something that sounded incredibly hilarious.

"What was that?"

"I think I'm—" he started, and then could not control it any longer. He watched himself heave out a mixture of mostly liquid, and a few French fries. Sardine slowly picked up her feet so as to not get her shoes covered with vomit. She didn't seem surprised. This was just another Tuesday, really. Trevor continued to heave a few more times, emptying his stomach of all possible toxic substances. Sardine kept one hand on her phone, and absentmindedly rubbed Trevor's back with the other. When a few caterers tried to rush down the empty hallway, Sardine screamed at them to take another route, again without looking up from her phone. Then another figure tried to walk down the hallway, and Sardine yelled once more.

"Get the hell out of here!" she screamed. But the figure did not, in fact, it kept moving toward them. "Can't you see this hallway is closed?!"

Trevor pitifully lifted his head to see the heavily lined face of someone he sort of recognized.

"Hello, Prince Trevor," the woman said.

"Hey . . . uh . . . " Trevor sputtered, trying to figure out which Aunt or Dame this was.

"Wszolek," the woman said. Trevor thought that maybe she had coughed, because that did not sound like a name.

"I'm sorry?" Sardine laughed. "Chohwl-heck?"

"Wszolek. President Wszolek," the woman said.

"President of what?" scoffed Sardine.

Trevor looked up at the woman and struggled to place her, without much success.

"Well, I'll see you out there, Prince," the President of the United States of America said as she walked away. When the door closed behind her, Sardine laughed.

"She was super rude," Sardine said.

"Yeah, I mean, am I supposed to remember *every* member of Congress or something?" Trevor asked. "On the plus side, I feel . . . so much better," he gasped. Sardine darted her eyes over to him from her phone, ever so briefly.

"Well you still look like shit," she announced. He did not care. He was ready for some food. He wearily rose to his feet, and stared at the puddle of vomit in front of him. He looked at Sardine, who shrugged once more. They quickly left without looking back. As they neared the majesty of the party outside, Trevor felt his resolve harden.

"I need to get back at Emma," he said.

"Mhmm," Sardine offered.

As he looked through the window and saw Vera darting across the field with rags in hand, he knew his target. He had seen the way Emma looked at her.

"Something she'll never forget," he said ominously.

Kyle was in the middle of a vastly boring conversation with some distant relative whose name he couldn't exactly remember. He rocked slowly back and forth as the Royal yacht floated its way around the Royal River that surrounded the Castle. He perched on the starboard railing, doing his best to pretend to pay attention and avoid catching the eye of the fourteen-year-old Glenn Hamilton, the younger brother of Tristan who often bullied Kyle, amongst others, for sport. Just as he saw Glenn trip an elderly woman with a plate of cheese and blame it on a caterer, he caught sight of her out of the corner of his eye. That toned leg, those chiseled arms, that confident smile—he would know Coach Nena anywhere. She was dressed in a stunningly sequined sports bra with matching athletic shorts, in costume as Sexy Fitness Coach, and deep in conversation with none other than weird Great-Uncle Rustbatham.

Kyle had not seen his Uncle Rusty since Christmas, when he was twenty pounds heavier and had long dark hair. Now that he had reappeared with a chiseled jaw and deeply tanned skin, he seemed to be able to get the attention of the elusive Coach Nena. Uncle Rusty was dressed in full Washingtonian garb and looked the part more than Kyle ever had. Also, there was a terrifying bird on his shoulder. Were women actually into that? Kyle made a mental note to look into training a hawk or two. At the very least he should get an eye patch, and maybe a parakeet.

"So I think I could really help you out," the man across from him said.

"Mhmm," Kyle responded, without actually listening.

"I've had a lot of patients who have the same problem, and let me tell you, this new drug will really cure you of all your problems. Yes, it's technically illegal, but I won't tell if you don't!" he said with a boisterous laugh. For the first time, Kyle looked at whom he was talking to. It was the Royal Doctor, Dr. McGilson.

"I'm sorry?" Kyle asked. Dr. McGilson leaned in and whispered loudly.

"The whole 'pooping too much' thing you Chattered. I can help you. And don't worry, I know how to pass all those pesky drug tests they'll put you on."

"Oh!" Kyle screeched. "Oh, no thank you. I have to go." He began to walk away quickly.

"Well you really should stop all that exercising!" Dr. McGilson yelled.

Kyle retreated to a far corner of the deck, away from anyone who would try to talk to him about the amount that he pooped. He cowered near the railing and looked down at his own Royal costume, the "Peasant Paperboy," and sighed heavily. He had loved being Peasant Paperboy ever since age five, and resolutely still wore the costume that had once fit his frail, youthful body. While Trevor dressed as a dashing and handsome George Washington, Kyle got to yell "Extra! Extra! Boston Tea Party is a Smash Hit!" during the entire night. He loved the line, but as he looked at his boyish attire and way-too-small costume, he wondered if perhaps this was not helping his game with Nena. He watched Uncle Rusty jealously for a few moments before deciding that he needed to take action into his own hands. If he couldn't talk to Coach Nena as himself, maybe he could talk to her as Sean, the poor peasant paperboy supporting his dying mother but dreaming of the big city.

"Hi, Kyle," came a tiny voice from below the punch table.

"It's Sean," Kyle said in his best poor paperboy accent, which was unfortunately not very good. He crawled under the punch table to find Miguel Jefferson, seven years old and a powerfully reclusive leader, sitting at his usual place. He was coincidentally also dressed as a paperboy.

"Right, sorry about that," Miguel answered as he sipped a glass of punch. Kyle struggled to fold his legs comfortably under the folding table. He always found himself most at home under the punch table during parties of this magnitude.

"So, Sean," Miguel asked slyly. "Will you be King tonight?"

"I cannot be King!" Kyle proclaimed in his most terrible accent. "I am but a poor peasant boy, bound by status and circumstance to work on the streets for the rest of my life!"

Miguel looked Kyle up and down, and then shook his head.

"You look stupid," he said brusquely.

"We're wearing the same outfit!" Kyle pointed out.

"Exactly," Miguel responded. "I'm seven."

Kyle shrugged, but was quickly distracted by his yearning heart once more.

"What do you do when you like a girl?" Kyle asked Miguel. He trusted Miguel implicitly; they had the same sort of "deer" spirit—eternally skittish, but gentle and kind at heart. Miguel seemed to know more about the world than Kyle felt he could ever possibly understand.

"Well," Miguel said, thinking deeply. "Usually I don't talk to her for many, many days."

"Check," Kyle responded.

"And then," Miguel continued. "Maybe at recess or something like that, I accidentally hit her with a ball, and then I have an excuse to talk to her. Once I gave a girl my juice box as an apology and she really liked that."

Kyle nodded, absorbing Miguel's wisdom. He had seen Trevor be mean to all the girls he had been with, and that had ended up working out very well for him. Kyle peeked his head out from under the punchbowl to see Trevor surrounded by throngs of Royal women in the very center of the strobe-lit deck, evidently telling a story that was very funny. It was like it didn't even matter that he had been seen in all of his Canadian-supporting glory. Oddly enough, Trevor was talking very closely to that maid of Emma's who looked sort of like a pleasant ghost. Kyle drew his head back in under the table to find Miguel staring at him with a concerned expression.

"Is everything okay, man?" Miguel asked.

Kyle shook his head. "I really like this girl and am afraid to talk to her."

Miguel nodded wisely, and patted Kyle on the knee. "Well, if you're King, it'll be a lot easier."

"What do you mean?"

Miguel shrugged and took another sip of his punch. "When you're King you can do whatever you want, and see whoever you want, and like whoever you want. That's what being a king is. For example, Donny is the King of second grade and he gets first pick at snack time."

Kyle felt Miguel's words wash over him and seep into his skin. If he was King, he could see Coach Nena *whenever* he wanted. He could have scribes write love letters and personal assistants craft phone messages and he could build an entire relationship without ever having to talk to her in person.

"I could do whatever I wanted," Kyle said softly under his breath.

"Yeah," Miguel answered. "But you probably

won't be King. There's no way he won't pick Trevor, and everyone thinks you're a stoner now."

Kyle's eyes narrowed, and his heart felt stronger than it ever had before. He had a goal; he had a mission. He was going to be King.

CHAPTER THIRTEEN

"**I**'m going to be King," Emma said to herself in the mirror once more. "I. Am. Going. To. Be. King." She looked herself in the eyes, nodded aggressively, and charged out of the bathroom to complete her mission. True, she had wounded Trevor with the bad press, but she wanted to truly *destroy* him with this one simple move. When she became King, she could not afford to have any sort of opposition. She marched across the boat deck, scanning for the face she knew would be hidden in the distance.

The party was an utter extravagance of Royal

proportions. Servers dressed in period garb darted around the massive boat, carrying platters of George Washington's favorite food and drink, like Madeira wine and Martha's famous leg of lamb recipe. Partygoers chatted and socialized, each sporting their own bizarre family heirloom, and showing off their status as best as they possibly could. Everyone wore his or her finest hats, sharpest boots, and most powdered wigs. Selfies snapped faster than Donna when the children were late. The RoyalChatterStream was flooded with the Royals' outfits and the peasant commentary on each and every juicy detail that Jane could eek out.

Duchess Sardine had to be in here somewhere, on one of these damn boats. Then, Emma's heart dropped when she saw Tristan Hamilton quickly approaching her out of the corner of her eye.

"Shit," she muttered under her breath. She turned around to find someone, anyone, to keep her safe, but it was too late.

"Emma!" he shouted when he was still way too far away.

"Tristan," Emma said, much less enthused.

"How's it going?" Tristan asked with a broad, stupid smile. Emma hated when boys smiled at her that way.

"Great," Emma said. She did not offer anything else, but Tristan was not deterred.

"I love your costume," he said.

"Thank you," Emma responded. Since all of her gowns were mysteriously ruined, Emma had chosen to wear full George Washington attire, powdered wig, waistcoat, and all. The silence stretched awkwardly between them. She had endured far too many of these conversations in her life to handle this one today. Just as she was about to fake a heart attack or a spider bite, she spotted the face she needed.

"Sardine!" she shouted to the distant figure of Duchess Sardine in the distance. Sardine looked around in confusion; nobody ever wanted to talk to her so aggressively. Emma looked at Tristan with a pained smile, and motioned to Sardine in the distance.

"Oh sure, I'll be right over!" she shouted. "Sorry, gotta run. Sardine calls."

"Burr," Tristan mumbled hatefully.

"Burr," Emma agreed, but she was already nearly out of conversation range.

"Catch you . . . later?" Tristan called after her.

"Definitely. Totally. Of course!" Emma shouted as she walked away from him to corner Duchess Sardine against the bar.

"Hey Duchess!" she said loudly, and Sardine seemed suspicious, at best.

"Hello?" Sardine responded. "What do you want?"

"Just wanted to check in, and see how you were doing!" Emma responded. "Can I get you a drink?"

Sardine narrowed her eyes at Emma.

"Why?"

"What do you mean, why?"

"Why do you want to get me a drink? We hate each other."

"Well, you're an important friend of my dear old brother, and I figured maybe it was time we got to know each other," Emma said cautiously. These next few steps could determine the course of her future. Then she saw Sardine's carefully guarded exterior crack just a little.

"We're not that close," Duchess Sardine said.

"What's wrong?" Emma asked, stepping closer toward Sardine. Sardine looked up at Emma with a brisk shrug.

"He's talking to some girl," Duchess Sardine said. Emma could tell Sardine wanted this conversation to end, but she could also see so clearly through Duchess Sardine's flimsy excuse for emotional distance.

"Tell me about it," Emma said, batting her eyes at Sardine to communicate she was on her side. "Whenever he finds a new girl, he doesn't need any of his friends, or even his sister anymore," she said.

"Exactly!" Sardine said with surprise. Emma smiled, and Sardine very nearly smiled back.

"And I'm sure it doesn't help that all of his friends are so mean to you all the time," Emma said soothingly.

"It's not fun," Sardine said with a biting laugh. Emma gently touched Sardine on the arm, and she did not jolt backwards—this game had basically already been won.

Four or five drinks later, Emma and Sardine were cackling in the far corner of the party, and Emma could feel that Trevor's total annihilation was within her power. She leaned in close to Sardine's plainly pretty face, and kissed her abruptly. Sardine looked back at her, eyes wide, and kissed her back. Before anyone could see, Emma jumped up and grabbed Sardine's hand. She led her off the boat and across the Royal Lawn to her favorite secluded spot in all of the gardens: the vine and fig trees. There was some dumb legend about Washingtons coming here to ponder life's greatest questions, but in reality, the Royal children just used it as a spot to hook up. Sardine giggled as Emma pulled her through the woods, and Emma dimly wondered where Vera was, and if she would care. But then the clearing of vine and fig trees were upon them, and Emma pulled Sardine into a shaded spot to continue the backstabbing of her brother. Although he wasn't romantically involved with Sardine, he most certainly considered her off limits to anyone and everyone around him—such was the nature of men who felt as if the world owed them everything they wanted. Emma could tell Trevor thought in the back of his mind that he might end up with Duchess Sardine one day, and she knew this would affect him deeply.

After a few minutes of the intense kind of tongue-tying that only a few drinks and a forbidden romance could provide, Emma heard the faint sounds of laughter and a low voice, not too far from them. She broke apart suddenly.

"What's wrong?" Sardine asked.

Emma shushed her. She continued to listen to the sounds, and could vaguely make out two voices that she knew by heart, but not yet by mind. She grabbed Sardine by the hand and charged through the clearing rather recklessly, and then she saw it. Her heart stopped cold. There, in the very same make-out grove, were Trevor and Vera, faces locked together.

"What the hell are you doing?" Emma asked. They broke apart and looked up at Emma and Sardine, hands firmly clasped.

"What the hell are *you* doing?" Trevor asked feebly. Sardine tried to let go of Emma's hand, but Emma held it tighter instinctively. As the knowledge washed over her that Trevor had chosen to get revenge in the very same fashion that she had, she calmly noted the crushing pain in her heart. She looked over at Vera, who seemed to be inching toward the edge of the clearing and blushing horribly. She looked over at Sardine, who refused to make eye contact. Finally, she looked at Trevor.

They locked eyes, and he nodded curtly. She nodded back. This round was a draw, and they may have ruined both of their love lives in the process. But alas, it was Royal warfare, what else could be expected?

King Jonathan paced backstage anxiously. He heard the distant yells and cheers from the reenactment unfolding on the SS Tea Party, as the crowds watched from the shore. From the sounds of it, they were getting closer to the climactic moment when all falls apart, and George Washington steps in to save the day and dump the tea. Of course this was not actually how the Boston Tea Party happened, but after years and years of historical reenactment parties in which George Washington was always the central figure, it was hard to keep track of what was fact and what was fiction. Most text books credited

George Washington with warning the Revolutionary forces that the British were coming, freeing the Slaves, and landing on the moon.

Jonathan knew his cue was on the horizon, and he knew the big announcement would be here soon enough. He would dump the tea overboard and then announce the climactic news that would change everything.

He wasn't ready.

He walked over to his horse, Buttercup XVIII. She was a majestic, black-haired beauty who radiated peace and calm. She was also a phenomenal horse actor and had been King Jonathan's trusted companion for every historical reenactment in his recent history. He placed a hand on Buttercup XVIII's head, and she looked at him with big, dark eyes. She snorted, and it blew his wig a little askew. He considered getting on Buttercup XVIII and riding away as far as he could. He glanced down at his GlassPhone™ and opened RoyalChatterStream reflexively. His heart nearly stopped in his chest when he saw the very first Direct Chatter from @JonathanLuvr452.

@JonathanLuvr452: Escape with me while you still can.

Another message appeared.

@JonathanLuvr452: Leave this kingdom behind. We can be:) together.

They *could* be smiley-face-together, and it was absolutely in his power.

Jonathan looked left, and looked right, and then climbed on top of Buttercup XVIII as gracefully as he could, which at his age and weight was not very graceful at all. Buttercup XVIII waited patiently until King Jonathan had safely mounted. She snorted once more, and he guided her toward the back ramp that connected to the fields behind them. Was this the sign he had been so desperately craving? As they reached the threshold of freedom, he saw the face of the woman he certainly did not want to see at a time like this.

"Hello, President," he said.

"Hello, King," Wszolek responded. "Happy retirement."

"Happy retirement to you, too," King Jonathan said, not so kindly. Wszolek's second term was nearly over, and soon she would be as irrelevant as President Nixon, who was maybe still down in the peasant section of the stocks.

"You know, I really tried," Wszolek said. "I really tried to make a difference. I wanted to change this Kingdom, and to make it better."

"You're in the wrong job for that," King Jonathan said with a snort.

"So are you," Wszolek responded. They eyed each other. "Well, the good news is that I get to retire. You, on the other hand . . . This will be your life forever. You'll never have any peace, or any freedom."

King Jonathan gulped. "When you're the King, you don't need freedom."

"Sure thing," Wszolek said, as she turned to walk away. "Happy birthday!"

As her haunting wish echoed in his ears, he considered the decision in front of him. He could run away right now to join @JonathanLuvr452, but it would only be a matter of time until the peasants, and the Stream, and his family found him. On the other hand, maybe there was another way out. Another option, one that would give him the freedom he desperately needed. He turned back to the stage and gallantly answered his cue.

Queen Donna had done it. She had gotten the entire family to the party, and put them in the right places at the right time. Now she just had to sit back and watch it unfold before her eyes. She watched as her husband pranced around with Buttercup XVIII onstage, making a big show of arriving just in time to dump all of the tea overboard. One by one,

Trevor, Kyle, and Emma filed out from backstage to join the audience. When King Jonathan announced his successor, the chosen child would march across the ornamental bridge and emerge onto the stage to join the play and by extension, the Kingdom.

Queen Donna eyed Kyle's ridiculous garb and Emma's utterly unacceptable costuming. Only Trevor looked remotely like a Washington should, but he also emanated the smell of sweaty feet and too much liquor. She gritted her teeth and said nothing as her stepchildren joined her. If everything went well, she would not have to deal with this kind of disobedience for much longer. Maybe she could even send them to Kentucky to live with their irrelevant mothers. She turned her attention back to the stage. King Jonathan dismounted his horse and addressed the rest of the Founding Fathers.

"My children," he said sagely. "Do not worry. Your fearless, dedicated leader, George Washington is here!" A round of applause echoed through the audience.

"We will not pay this tax!" he shouted. "Dump the tea!"

Everyone cheered loudly, and the tea was hauled over the edge of the boat and dumped into the river. Next to Donna, she could feel the children's hearts racing and their pulses pounding. She almost felt bad for them. Almost.

On cue, the Thomas Jefferson impersonator slowly raised his hand.

"Sir," Jefferson said. "We accept you as our leader for the rest of time! We only have one more question. Who will be King after you?"

For a few moments, nobody made a sound. This was the line at which King Jonathan would change the course of the nation. He had been named King in this fashion, and his father before him. Donna leaned in as the silence stretched longer.

"Sir?" the Jefferson impersonator asked again. King Jonathan looked blankly out into the audience, and he heard the continuous snapping of pictures as the reporters sensed that something was amiss.

"Who will be King next?" the Jefferson imperson-ator asked once more, lamely. King Jonathan walked very slowly from the far end of the stage, over to the other end. He looked up into the glaring lights and then out at the people stretched before him.

Finally, King Jonathan opened his mouth, and a croaky sound emerged. "The next King will be . . . " he said slowly, as if the words did not fit correctly. "Will be . . . " King Jonathan repeated. "Will be . . . me," he finally said. For what seemed to be an eternity, nobody spoke. Then, Jefferson coughed lightly.

"Excuse me, sir?"

"I said that the next King will be me," King Jonathan repeated. A terse whisper of confusion rip-pled through the throngs of Royals. Next to Donna, she felt the children each tense as if they had been electrocuted. She relished their suffering.

"Order! Order!" King Jonathan yelled when the whispers had grown into a dull roar. The crowd reluctantly quieted down.

"Due to a handwritten, never-before-seen footnote in the Constitution, I will not be turning over the crown tonight," he declared. "Article 15, Section X reads as follows," he said, as he pulled out the very scroll Donna had procured.

"If none of the Royal heirs are married, and if the Royal King does not feel comfortable passing on the Crown to an unwed heir, he may delay the coronation on his sixty-fifth birthday, for three months," he said. As soon as he finished speaking the reporters launched into utter frenzy.

"That is my Royal decree," Jonathan said with finality. "None of my children will be King tonight. I will revisit the issue in three months' time, or when there is a Royal wedding."

Queen Donna felt her anxieties melt away as she watched her husband leave the stage. He wasn't the smartest, or the cleverest, but he would certainly follow his stupid heart to the ends of the earth, even when the object of his desire was a ChatterStream love that he had never met. She turned to face the shell-shocked offspring, each of whom seemed unable to speak. She surveyed them with a sick satisfaction. Finally, they had nothing to say.

"Well," Queen Donna said, with a slight smile. "I guess we might need to start planning some weddings."